About the author

Linda Newbery taught English in various schools before becoming a full-time author, and a regular tutor of writing courses for children and adults.

She has written a number of books for young adults, and has been three times nominated for the Carnegie Medal, as well as for the Writers Guild Award.

Linda lives in Northamptonshire with her husband and three cats.

The *Moving On* trilogy by Linda Newbery

No Way Back
Break Time
Windfall

ORCHARD BOOKS
96 Leonard Street, London EC2A 4XD
Orchard Books Australia
Unit 31/56 O'Riordan Street, Alexandria, NSW 2015
First published in Great Britain in 2002
A PAPERBACK ORIGINAL
Text © Linda Newbery, 2002
The right of Linda Newbery to be identified as the
author of this work has been asserted by her
in accordance with the Copyright,
Designs and Patents Act, 1988.
A CIP catalogue record for this book is
available from the British Library.
ISBN 1 84121 586 4
1 3 5 7 9 10 8 6 4 2
Printed in Great Britain

WINDFALL

Linda Newbery

ORCHARD BOOKS

For Jean Ure
– at last!

Bad Monday

Today was going to be trouble. Nathan had that feeling.

For starters, he hadn't done his weekend homework. That was nothing out of the ordinary, but this time he'd been given an ultimatum by his Year Head. Homework had been the last thing on Nathan's mind over the weekend; he hadn't wanted to stay at home any more than he had to. It was only when Mr Kershaw walked into the form-room that Nathan remembered he was supposed to have all his books ready for inspection, and his homework diary signed by Mum to say he'd done it all. That was a laugh – the idea of Mum noticing whether he'd done his homework or not, or bothering to look in his diary.

It was quite likely that Mr Kershaw would have forgotten all about it too, if it hadn't been for that obnoxious Natalie girl calling out, 'Done your

History, Nathe?' That was deliberate. Everything Natalie did was aimed at getting someone else into trouble or herself out of it.

'Oh, yes,' Mr Kershaw said, in the sort of voice that meant he'd rather have forgotten. 'You'd better bring it here, Nathan, and let me have a look.'

'Haven't done it, have I?' Nathan said. There was no point pretending.

Nearly everyone was listening now. It was a knack Nathan had, quite unintentionally. There was something about his tone of voice when he answered teachers back. Everyone wanted to see how far into trouble he'd get himself. Usually he obliged them by getting ruder and ruder, stomping out of the room or kicking something. But he was rarely rude to Steve Kershaw; offhand, yes, but not openly rude. Mr Kershaw was a PE teacher, youngish, quite easy-going, only chasing Nathan now because various other teachers had got on to him. He gave you the sense of being on your side, even when he told you off.

'Come here, Nathan.' Steve Kershaw pulled up another chair beside his own at the teacher's desk. He wasn't going to let the whole form listen.

Nathan ambled up to the front.

'You know Mrs Reynolds is going to ask me about this,' Mr Kershaw said. He sighed, looking at the report card he was supposed to fill in for Nathan each morning about the previous night's homework. 'You do like to make life difficult for yourself, don't you? What was it this time?'

'Dunno,' Nathan mumbled. 'Forgot.'

Mr Kershaw looked at him in exasperation. He wore a polo shirt and track pants and was tanned from being out on the football or athletics pitches. He reminded Nathan a bit of his dad – once Nathan had called him Dad by mistake, and had been ragged about it for days by Reado and the others. Steve Kershaw was a good bit younger than Dad, but he was a dad himself. His kid was only a baby, not a year old yet. He'd brought in photos to show them, all proud.

Nathan couldn't imagine his own dad passing round photographs. Dad hardly remembered that Nathan existed, except for the odd weekend when it suited him.

'I can understand people forgetting to do their homework now and then,' Steve Kershaw was saying. 'But we're not talking about *now and then*, are we? We're talking about nearly every night. Do yourself a favour, Nathan, and sort yourself out. I'm going to have to pass this card on to Mrs Reynolds and she's bound to want to see you herself. Did you forget *all* your homework, or just the History?'

'All of it,' Nathan said.

Truth was, he hadn't given school a thought from leaving on Friday afternoon until dragging himself out of bed this morning. To him, school was just something he had to get through every day, spending the required number of hours there until the bell released him at three-thirty. Sometimes he found ways of spending less than the required hours. It wouldn't bother him if he never went at all. Why should it be imposed on him? He hadn't asked for a place at school, had he? He wasn't interested in exams and qualifications. He didn't even care much which Options he took next year, though somehow that had all been sorted out. Why did all these teachers have rights over his time, his life? It wasn't as if Mum could care less what he did. All she wanted was for him to stay out of trouble so that his teachers would leave her alone.

Only problem was, he couldn't quite manage that.

'Best thing I can suggest,' Mr Kershaw said, 'is that you start on some of it now. The Maths, say. You can sit in the PE office. You've got ten minutes. At least that might be enough to get you out of trouble with *one* of your teachers. And then I'll have to find out when Mrs Reynolds can see you.'

Nathan said nothing. He went back to his place, kicked Damien's bag under the table, found his dog-eared Maths books and left the mobile classroom. He might do some of the Maths. Or he might not.

Later, confronted by Mrs Reynolds, he had to admit that it would have been a good idea to do what Mr Kershaw had told him, rather than wander off across the sports field.

'Ten minutes' *work*, he told you,' Mrs Reynolds fired at him. She had him in her office now, and had sat him down on a chair by her desk – the door was firmly closed and there was no escape. 'Not ten minutes off to do whatever you liked. What were you doing over there by the trees? Having a fag?'

'No!' Nathan took an interest in the conversation for the first time. Smoking was one thing he didn't do. It wasn't fair! Just because he bunked off and didn't get his homework done, they thought they could accuse him of *anything*. Old Reynolds probably hoped he'd start dealing in illegal substances – then she could have him excluded and get shot of him altogether.

'Look, Nathan.' Mrs Reynolds' voice took on a resigned tone. 'I've tried to be fair. I've tried this homework report and it's just not working. *You're* not working, not even pretending to. And disobeying Mr Kershaw as well – you don't leave me much choice, do you? You're on detention tonight and on

Blue Card all week. That means being on time, having the books you need and doing the work set. Well, you know all that. Don't forget to give it to the teacher every lesson, to be signed. You'll be on it next week as well if you don't buck your ideas up. And you can spend lunchtime in here, catching up on your weekend homework.'

Nathan slumped in the chair, saying nothing, not looking at her.

'Did something happen this weekend, Nathan?' Mrs Reynolds asked, her expression friendlier. 'Did you see your dad?'

'No!' he flared again. What business was it of hers, what he did at weekends, who he saw?

Afterwards, he could have kicked himself. If he'd said yes, he'd seen Dad, she'd have come over all sympathetic and understanding. He could blame anything on seeing Dad. But for some reason he made it a point of honour not to lie to her or Mr Kershaw. Answer in grumpy monosyllables, refuse to speak at all, stomp out and slam the door behind him – those were his tactics. But something stopped him from lying about Dad.

'I shall have to phone home, to explain about this.' Mrs Reynolds handed him the new report card, all marked off in squares, one for each lesson of the week, with spaces for the teachers to sign and make comments. Nathan had seen plenty of them before. It was time for the next lesson; he heard the swell of voices and movement in the corridor outside. 'And do try to stay out of trouble for the rest of the day, will you? Do yourself a favour,' Mrs Reynolds finished, with a smile, or at least an effort at a smile.

Nathan went out into the corridor, stuffing the report card into his pocket. Teachers were always telling him to do himself a favour. Why couldn't they do themselves a favour – shut up and leave him alone? He wasn't exactly *trouble*some. He didn't start fights or try to be a smart-arse or act up in class the way Natalie did. He only got into trouble when teachers started on him.

Damien was coming towards him, taking up the whole width of the corridor with a huge sports bag slung over his shoulder, so that little Year Sevens had to duck out of his way. He punched Nathan on the arm. 'All right, Nathe? What happened in there – d'you get done again?'

'Blue Card.' Nathan pulled it out from his pocket. 'And a phone call home.'

Damien whistled. 'You must be top scorer for Blue Cards, you know that? Going for the *Guinness Book of Records*, or what?'

'Don't bother me,' Nathan said, though this wasn't

strictly true. The phone call home was no problem –
Mum probably wouldn't even mention it, or if she
did, she'd only say, 'That Year Head woman rang
again. Can't you *try* to stay out of trouble?' and leave
it at that. The Blue Card was a bigger nuisance,
because you had to get it signed by a teacher for every
lesson, and if there was a single bad comment – *Did
no work* or *Came without exercise book* – you'd get
an after-school detention. Nathan sometimes wished
he lived far enough from school to travel on the bus,
like lots of people did, instead of only half a mile
away – it was too easy for Mrs Reynolds to keep him
in. Tonight, straight after school, Nathan had
planned on getting the bus into town – it was market
day and he thought he'd help Smudge for a bit. He
wasn't going home till he had to, not with the mood
Mum had been in.

They sauntered down to Maths, overtaken by some
of the girls from their form.

'Have you heard? Jo's leaving at the end of term?'
Judith was telling someone.

'Leaving, why?' the other girl asked.

'She's moving up to Yorkshire with her mum,'
Judith said.

Damien pushed past and went to bag the seat at the
back where he wasn't usually allowed to sit. Nathan
lingered in the doorway in case Judith was going to

say any more, but the group of girls split up and went to their places.

Jo, leaving! How could she? Just when—

'Hey, let us past!' Reado, from behind, prodded Nathan in the small of the back. Not bothering to retaliate, Nathan shoved past Samantha Warburton, dumped his bag and sat down with his legs stretched out in the gangway, where Samantha promptly tripped over them as she made her way to her table.

'*Move*, can't you, you gangling great lump?' she said, glaring.

Nathan didn't answer. He scowled at his desktop, gloomier than ever. Nothing was going right today.

Sanctuary

'It's not as if you can't *do* the work.' Mr O'Shaughnessy had an unpleasant way of thrusting his head towards you, shoving his face about two inches from yours, so close that you could see the red veins in his cheeks and the hairs in his nose, if you looked. Nathan didn't look. It was easier to stare at the wall and pretend that the tirade was directed at someone else.

'It's not as if you're *stupid*—'

Being stupid would be quite OK, then, would it? Teacher logic was hard to follow sometimes.

Mr O'Shaughnessy threw Nathan's exercise book down on the desk in a gesture of disgust. 'You're just idle, Fuller.' Mr O'Shaughnessy was one of those old-fashioned teachers who called boys, but not girls, by their surnames. '*Bone* idle.'

Nathan had heard the phrase applied to himself before. For the first time it struck him what an odd idea it was. *Bone idle* seemed to be worse than merely *idle.* But what did bones have to do with it? He pictured a skeleton, a pile of bones lying in a heap. Skeletons were entitled to be idle, weren't they? What did people expect them to do, get up and dance about, like in that song about the foot bone connecting to the leg bone?

Besides, he *had* done some work during the lesson. Mr O'Shaughnessy was still going on about the missing homework, so Nathan didn't expect any credit for the little he'd done in the last hour. He didn't mind Maths, not in the lessons, anyway. He had enough native wit to get by, even if he didn't listen very hard when Mr O'Shaughnessy was explaining.

'I'll give you ten minutes to eat your lunch, then I want you back here doing your homework,' Mr O'Shaughnessy was saying. 'That'll give you forty minutes.'

'Can't,' Nathan said. 'Seeing Miss Reynolds.'

Mr O'Shaughnessy glared. '*I* can't, *Sir. I'm* seeing *Mrs* Reynolds,' he corrected. 'Is it too much trouble for you to speak in sentences? Or can you only spare the odd syllable? Well,' he went on, as Nathan gave no answer, 'since you have such a full diary of pressing engagements, I shall obviously have to make an appointment with you for later in the week. Tomorrow lunchtime. Promptly at ten past. Make a note of it in your social calendar, could you?'

Nathan turned to go. Mr O'Shaughnessy always wittered on in that sarcastic way. You just had to wait till he stopped. Presumably, he wanted to have his own lunch.

But Mr O'Shaughnessy hadn't finished. 'Did you hear me?'

'Yes,' Nathan said, still heading for the door. 'Sir.'

Much practised, Nathan could make *Sir* sound far more insolent than not saying it at all. He got out of the classroom at last, remembered that he hadn't brought any lunch and decided to look for Damien to see if he could scrounge some food – he could always tell Mrs Reynolds that Mr O'Shaughnessy had kept him in. It was the summer term now and everyone was supposed to be outside. Younger kids were chasing each other around on the grass, older ones sitting in groups under the trees, others heading off for the farther corners of the field, where the clear view of duty staff approaching gave plenty of time to stub out cigarettes. Damien was more than likely to be over there, but on the way Nathan saw Jo, who was on her own heading for the tennis courts, swinging her racquet. He remembered what Judith had said about Jo leaving. There was something he wanted to put right, something that had been bothering him since last term.

He accelerated so that his path crossed hers, and stopped in front of her.

'Hi, Nathan,' she said, still swinging the racquet in a backhanded swipe. Jo was one of the few girls in the form who had time for Nathan, and she was the only girl he liked. Not that he fancied her or wanted to go out with her or anything like that. She was all right, Jo. She wasn't daft like most girls were, clustering in cliques and whispering behind their hands and then giggling loudly so you'd know they were talking about you. She was small and tough and energetic. Though she never got into trouble the way he did, he thought of her as a possible ally, since the Outdoor Pursuits trip.

'You know that dog,' he said straight away.

'What dog?' Baffled brown eyes looked at him from under a fringe.

'You know.' He lowered his voice, even though there was no one near enough to hear. 'That dog I told you about. That time in English.'

'Oh yes! Your dog. He's got a funny name. Gaz, isn't it? What's happened to him?' She looked worried for a moment, perhaps expecting him to say Gaz had died or been run over.

'Nothing. There isn't a dog. I haven't really got a dog. I made it up.'

Jo stared. Nathan saw Damien out of the corner of

his eye, walking across the field with Jason and Eduardo, making grabs at a big bag of crisps Eduardo was holding. Nathan was already regretting the impulse for honesty that had made him approach Jo. She must think he was off his trolley.

But 'Oh,' was all she said. She didn't seem particularly surprised; maybe she expected him to tell lies all the time. He felt hurt by that.

'Judith says you're leaving. Going to Yorkshire.' There was always a chance Jo might deny it, say it was rubbish. 'How soon you going?'

She started swishing her racquet again. 'Oh, not till the summer holidays. There's things to sort out. Look, I've got to meet Lynette. She's over there already.' Then, about to walk off briskly – Jo was always in a hurry to get somewhere or other – she paused, and added, 'You'd really like a dog, though, wouldn't you – one of your own? They've got dogs at that sanctuary place – you know? – the one in Coldharbour Lane. Dogs that need homes. See you later.'

She jogged on towards the tennis courts, and Nathan walked over to join Damien. If Jo wasn't leaving till the end of term, he needn't have told her yet. It had been in an English lesson last term; Mr Barrington had had some batty idea about them interviewing each other, and he'd been paired up with

Jo. That was all right – the questions were the trouble. The whole idea had been to *find out* about people – private, personal things about home lives and dreams and ambitions. Just so that they could pretend to be journalists and write up daft interviews with each other, as if they were all famous. He'd made up this story about having a dog called Gaz, just for something to say, to direct the conversation away from the areas he didn't want to discuss. Jo had believed it all right; she'd seemed interested, and asked him to bring in a photo. Since then he hadn't liked to tell her there was no such dog, no dog at all.

Jo wasn't daft; she knew why he'd lied. A dog of his own, that was what Nathan wanted. With his own dog, nothing else would seem quite so bad. But it was no good knowing there were dogs that needed homes at this sanctuary place. That only made it worse. Dogs needed homes and Nathan needed a dog, but there was no chance of him having one at home, no chance at all. For a few moments, as he sauntered over towards Damien, he considered getting a very, very small dog, and smuggling it into the bedroom he shared with his brother, smuggling it out every day for walks. But that wouldn't do. He didn't want a small dog, a fluffy yappy thing like Elfie next door, who sat in the front window like an ornament and wore a pink bow in her hair, and a knitted coat when she went out in winter. He wanted a big lollopy dog, something tough and waggy and full of energy, with a plumy tail and a laughing face – a real dog. He'd had a dog once, years ago, when Dad had still been at home – Prince, a rough collie. But after Prince died, Mum wouldn't get another one. 'This house is too small,' she said, or 'I haven't got time for looking after dogs,' or even 'They dig up the garden.' That was a joke. You'd think their garden was the sort of thing you saw on telly, all designer gravel, instead of a trodden patch of grass with a few bits of shrub round the edges.

Dad had been the one who liked dogs. When they moved to a bigger house, he'd told Nathan, then they'd get one. But Dad was the one who had moved. On his own.

'Got anything to eat, Dame?' Nathan asked as he approached. 'You haven't scoffed the lot? I'm starving!'

Eduardo handed him half a cheese roll and Jason passed over a stick of chewing gum. It was only when the bell went for afternoon registration that Nathan remembered he was supposed to have spent lunchtime in Mrs Reynolds' office.

Grounded

By the time Nathan got into town, to the car park that became a market on Mondays and Saturdays, Smudge was about to start packing up the stall.

'Bit quiet today, since lunchtime.' Smudge lit up a fag and handed the packet to Nathan, who refused. 'Still, if you could hang on here for half an hour, there's a bloke I want to see about a new load of stuff.'

Nathan shrugged. It suited him to mind the stall for a bit, then wander round the market when Smudge came back. Smudge's partner, Trev, was nowhere to be seen. Probably doing business somewhere. *Doing business* was what he and Smudge called it, although as far as Nathan could tell, it was business of a doubtful kind. Trev and Smudge sold cassette tapes and CDs, at half the prices you'd pay in shops. 'Don't ask, little bruv,' was all Smudge would say, when Nathan asked where he got them from. 'Little bruv' was getting to be a joke, now that Nathan was a good bit taller than Smudge. Smudge, who was eighteen now, had stopped growing at fourteen, though his cheerful toughness, aggressively short haircut and quick tongue made up for his lack of height. He'd left school before taking any exams and had been earning his way, buying and selling things at various markets, ever since.

Nathan sold a couple of CDs to two girls from the Year above him at school. He didn't know whether they recognised him or not. Sometimes, though he couldn't be bothered today, he imitated Smudge's manner, laughing and joshing the customers in a sort of endless talking without saying much, knocking off an extra fifty pence if he thought it would result in a sale. That was how Smudge had met his girlfriend Cheryl, selling her a CD. One of the bonuses that went with the job, Smudge called it. Today, anything Nathan sold at all would be a bonus, since the stall was about to shut down. It was a warm afternoon, late-April-nearly-May, and if it weren't for the rumbling in his stomach there would be no reason to go home for a few hours yet.

'Hi, Nathan,' the woman at the next stall called to him. 'Helping your brother?'

Nathan nodded, the answer being obvious. He didn't know the woman's name, though she was always there, every market day, standing squarely with arms folded over a large chest and a stomach that bulged under a T-shirt. He rarely saw her sell anything, and wondered why she bothered – people weren't exactly queuing up to buy velvet cushion covers with tassels, nylon sheets or fancy bits of cord for tying curtains back.

'Here you go, Nathe. Got you this.' Smudge was back, handing over a burger wrapped in a paper napkin, and a can of Coke.

'Great! Thanks, bruv.' Nathan took a huge bite, burning his tongue on the hot meat and onions, in case Smudge might change his mind and grab it back. He could easily have eaten three or four.

'Ent you had nothing to eat today?' Smudge was eating his own burger more slowly, raising a hand to wipe tomato sauce from his lips.

'Didn't have any cash, did I?'

'Here. I can give you a couple of quid.' Smudge rummaged in the bum bag he used for carrying cash, and handed over two pound coins, then a third. His takings didn't amount to vast sums, but Nathan knew that he quite liked playing the magnanimous elder brother, handing out burgers and dosh. Also, it made sure that Nathan kept coming along to help.

'Thanks. You going home after this?' Nathan hoped so. From the way Smudge breezed in and out, you'd have thought everything was normal, and most people's homes were like theirs.

Smudge grinned. 'No. Seeing Cheryl. Her place.' He pronounced it *Chel*. 'And no, you can't come too.'

'Why'd I want to?' Nathan licked up a last fragment of onion from his napkin and threw the screwed-up paper in the rubbish box behind the stall. 'Cheryl's a stupid bimbo.'

'Yeah. But let me tell you, mate, there are compensations.' Smudge grinned again, man-to-man. 'She's got friends, if you're interested. I'll say you're sixteen.'

'No thanks.'

'Anyway, I 'spect you got homework to do. Well, I'm about to pack up.' Smudge tossed his burger wrapping on to the pavement, stretched and yawned. 'Don't know where Trev's got to.'

'Don't ask,' Nathan mimicked.

Most of the tapes and CDs were displayed in boxes, so it took only a few minutes to stack everything in Trev's van. 'See you Friday,' Smudge called as he drove off. 'Be good.'

Nathan wandered around the market for a while, spending some of Smudge's money on a bar of chocolate and another Coke. He liked looking around the stalls, but today, with the detention and a final earwigging from Mrs Reynolds, he'd arrived a bit late; most stallholders were already packing up. Several of them knew him by sight, and the bloke at the cheese counter gave him a pork pie. Then he helped Stan at the fruit and veg stall to pack up, and earned another two pounds. Not bad.

He went into the park and ate his pork pie by the lake, throwing crumbs to the ducks. Afterwards, he sat on one of the swings for a while, ignoring a young woman with two small children who kept looking pointedly at the notice which said *This playground is for use only by children under fourteen.* Nathan *was* fourteen, even if not under, but the woman obviously didn't think he had swinging rights; maybe she thought he'd attack her little kids or something. After a while, bored by staying put just to make the point that he could sit there if he wanted, he got up and left, kicking an empty Coke can across the playground, and thought of going round to Damien's.

Damien's house wasn't far from the park, in a neat estate of semi-detached houses with clean cars parked outside, sometimes two to a house. The gardens were carefully tended, with lots of tulips and flowering stuff, and the man next door to Damien's was out mowing his grass. Damien's house had a brand new porch with one of those urn things in front, full of stunted tulips, and the door had a big brassy knocker that looked like it belonged to some great mansion.

It was Damien's mum who answered. She was wearing a flowery dress and make-up, and the smell of cooking wafted out as she opened the door – something spicy, like spaghetti sauce. She didn't look too pleased to see Nathan. Nathan knew that he wasn't the sort of boy she liked Damien hanging around with.

'Damien in?' he asked, matching her stony expression.

'Yes, but he can't come out. He's grounded all this week, didn't he tell you? He's upstairs doing his homework.'

She gave Nathan a penetrating look that implied he should be at home doing his, too.

'I'll tell him you called round. You can see him at school tomorrow.'

'Yeah, right,' Nathan muttered to the closed door. He aimed a desultory kick at the terracotta urn, then saw that Damien's mum was waiting behind the net-curtained window to make quite sure he left the premises. He pushed his hands into his pockets and ambled down the path, to show that he'd go at his own speed. Snidey cow. Still, he could give Dame some stick tomorrow about being grounded, about sitting up there in his bedroom dutifully doing his homework. Damien hadn't said a word about that. He liked to show the same contempt for teachers and school rules as Nathan did, but there was a key difference. Damien could get away with only so much before his parents stepped in – they were the sort of parents who'd check his homework diary and phone the school and keep Damien shut up in his room till he'd got all his work done. It meant that Damien had a sort of safety-net – he could go so far and then give in, blaming his parents, calling them tight, unfair, Fascists. Nathan had no safety-net, not with Dad gone. He could do exactly as he liked and no one would know. But that didn't give him the sense of freedom he might have expected. It only filled him with a sort of hopelessness. Nothing he did mattered. No one cared.

It was with that feeling of surrender that he walked towards home. His was a few streets away from Damien's, past a parade of shops with flats above them. The house was one of a semi-detached pair beyond the last shop, a newsagent's. Next door they'd made a bit of an effort with a new panelled door, a carriage lamp, and blinds at the windows. Nathan's front garden was just a little square of grass with a concrete path. The daffodils that grew in a straight line beside the path – Dad had put those in, his one and only attempt at gardening – had faded into brown crispy flower heads that no one had bothered to pick off.

Nathan let himself in.

The front door led straight into the main room. The curtains were drawn. Mum was on the sofa, watching TV, her legs curled up. She looked round at Nathan in what he thought of as her half-dead way, like someone only partly conscious. The room smelled of cigarette ash and the coffee-table was ringed with stains where mugs had stood.

'Where've you been?' she asked him, from her trance.

'Helping Smudge. It's Monday, remember?'

'I suppose he'll be in in a minute wanting his dinner.' Mum reached out for her cigarette packet and lighter. 'There's a pizza in the fridge. Stick it under the grill, will you?'

'I don't want anything,' Nathan said, though he had felt hungry enough outside Damien's house. 'And Smudge ent coming back. He's going round Cheryl's.'

'Fine. Saves me the bother. Put the kettle on, will you? I'm dying for a cup of tea.' Mum lit up and sank back into the sofa cushions. Nathan glanced at the screen to see what she was watching. Nothing he recognised; probably something she'd videoed. He went into the kitchen, made two mugs of tea – tea-bags in mugs, two spoonfuls of sugar in each, a slosh of milk and a quick stir round – and carried them both through.

Mum took hers without speaking, her eyes still on the screen. Her fair hair was unbrushed, hanging in tangles each side of her face, and her eyes were still smudged with Saturday night's make-up. Nathan waited a few moments to see if she was going to say anything about Mrs Reynolds phoning, but she seemed to have forgotten he was in the room.

He took his mug of tea up to his room, turned on the radio and closed the door.

Nadia

Mum hadn't always been like this. Nathan could remember her being bright, busy, concerned about her appearance, cooking meals and doing the shopping, like other people's mums. Even after Dad had gone. *Especially* after Dad had gone; at first she'd seemed to become younger, going out with friends, talking endlessly on the phone, like a teenager. You'd have thought Dad had been nothing but a nuisance, stopping her from leading her own life.

There had been boyfriends. Doug. Rob. Brian. Nathan hadn't liked it at first – he used to worry about what would happen if Dad came back – but gradually he got used to it: Mum not coming home at night, or a strange man staying in the house. Brian had lasted longer than the others, and Nathan had begun to recognise a routine – Brian coming over on Friday and Tuesday nights, going to bed with Mum, then leaving at two or three in the morning, letting himself out. Sometimes he'd come over at odd times, too, Saturday or Sunday lunchtimes. He came straight from the pub, smelling of beer and stale cigarette ash. He'd come in flushed and cheerful, bringing Mum flowers or chocolates, tickling and teasing her, joking with Nathan.

Sometimes Brian and Mum went upstairs then, in the middle of the afternoon. Nathan pretended not to know what they were doing. Brian was a big man, with dark curly hair, a fat chin with a roll of flesh underneath, and a big laugh. In his after-pub moods, he'd sometimes play-wrestle with Nathan. Often it was like wrestling a big friendly bear, but sometimes there was a threat beneath the play that made Nathan realise how easily Brian could overpower him. Nathan went along with the play-fighting, though he never started it himself. He was never sure that it wouldn't turn into real fighting, fighting to hurt.

Then suddenly, about eight months ago, Brian didn't come any more. Nathan remembered Mum waiting for him in the front room on Friday night, a bottle of wine open and a meal cooking in the oven, going dry. Mum had ended up drinking the whole bottle herself. Next morning, red-eyed and snivelly in her dressing gown, she threw the dried-up food in the dustbin.

She could have put it down on the grass for the

birds to eat, Nathan thought. But Mum wasn't in the mood for criticism.

She never mentioned Brian again. Nadia said, when Nathan asked her, 'His wife found out.'

Nathan was shocked, though he could have worked out for himself that Brian had a wife – kids too, Nadia said. Brian must have told all sorts of lies, sneaking out of the house to see Mum. This explained why he had never stayed the whole night. He must have pretended he'd been out with mates, going home in the early hours. Nathan thought of that other family, Brian's family, not knowing what their dad was up to, all that time. He wondered whether Brian had a son, a boy he wrestled with. If so, that boy was luckier – at least he'd got his dad back. Nathan's dad wasn't coming back.

Nathan lay on his bed staring at the ceiling and listening to music. One advantage of sharing a room with Smudge was that there was a ready supply of new cassettes and CDs. Nathan sometimes sold them at school, when Smudge was feeling generous. The house felt empty without Smudge. Now that he'd got Cheryl, he went round to her house several evenings a week. He got fed there, he'd told Nathan, by Cheryl's mum. At Cheryl's house they had great big meals: meat and potatoes and Yorkshire, steak and kidney pudding, mounds of mashed potato, apple pies and custard. It'd be almost worth putting up with Cheryl for that, Nathan thought, and the chance to be in a normal house where people talked to each other. All right for Smudge.

A door slammed downstairs and voices were raised: Nadia had come. Nathan went down.

The baby buggy was parked at the bottom of the stairs, taking up most of the space. He edged round it and went into the front room. Nadia was standing there, facing Mum, holding the baby, Katy, in her arms. She had opened the curtains so that sunlight flooded in, showing up the dust and the cigarette ash all over the coffee-table, the fluff and dirt on the carpet.

'Come on, Mum,' Nadia was saying. 'We're going to get this place tidied up. It's not fit for a pig. No wonder Smudge goes round to that girlfriend's as much as he can. D'you want him to leave home altogether?'

Mum stood up slowly, brushing flakes of ash off her sweatshirt. Jolted out of the film she'd been watching, she stared at Nadia as if she couldn't quite remember who she was.

'You can start by putting the shopping away,' Nadia bossed.

'Nathan'll do it.' Mum's eyes swam up to his face, focusing slowly. 'Won't you, love?'

'You all right, Nathan?' Nadia asked him. 'Everything all right at school?'

'Yeah,' Nathan said.

'No, it's not. He's been getting himself in trouble. They phoned today,' Mum said, sitting down again. 'He's not been doing his homework.'

'I'm not surprised he hasn't,' Nadia said hotly. 'Put the shopping away, Nathan, then we'll get some tea.'

'Isn't Owen coming?' Nathan asked. He liked Owen.

'No, he's helping someone fix a car. He'll see you at the weekend,' Nadia said, handing him two Sainsbury's bags. 'Careful, there's eggs in there.'

Nathan carried the shopping into the kitchen. 'He said he wasn't hungry—' he heard Mum say, but then Nadia cut in, 'Honestly, Mum, do you want him to end up in Care?'

She'd lowered her voice, not intending Nathan to hear, but he heard anyway. He left the shopping and stood by the half-open door, listening.

'He's old enough to look after himself,' Mum was saying, in the whiney voice she used when Nadia bossed her.

'No, he's not. He's only fourteen. He might look older but he's just a kid. You've got to make more effort, Mum! You should have kept that appointment with the doctor.'

'I'm not going back there, Nads,' Mum argued. 'I know what he'll say. "It's all in your mind. Get out more, take an interest in things."' She put on a posh voice, mimicking the doctor.

'Well, he's right,' Nadia retorted.

'It's easy to say that—'

'You could at least *go*—'

Nadia's voice was moving towards the kitchen. Hastily, Nathan bent to pick up the supermarket carrier bag, and looked inside to see what she had bought. A packet of ham, two tins of baked beans. Six eggs, a loaf of bread and a wedge of cheese. At least now he could make himself some lunch for tomorrow.

Nadia came in and started clearing up: tidying things into the sink, running hot water, breaking eggs for an omelette. She brought the baby in, asking Nathan to keep an eye on her. Katy was a good-natured baby, her eyes following Nathan as he knelt on the floor and dangled one of her fluffy toys and waggled his fingers to make her laugh. Every so often she'd smile, a wide toothless smile, for some reason finding Nathan tremendously funny.

It had seemed like a family disaster when Nadia got pregnant with Katy, but now Katy was one of the best things that had happened to them. If Nathan couldn't have a dog of his own, he could have a part-share in

Katy and that was nearly as good. He was her uncle, Nadia had pointed out. Uncle Nathan. It made him feel odd, but proud. Not many people his age were uncles.

'She's always good with you,' Nadia said, at the sink.

Nathan liked it when Nadia came round. She was twenty-one, short and stocky like Smudge, with more energy than the rest of the family combined. Nads, Mum always called her. Typical of Mum to give her a really classy name like Nadia – like a Russian ballerina or gymnast – then shorten it to Nads. They were all 'N's, except Dad, whose name was Barry. Mum was Nina, usually shortened to Neen. Nigel, Smudge's real name, had been abandoned from the age of eleven. Nathan supposed that all those 'N's had been meant to make them sound like a real family, belonging together. Perhaps that was what they had been, once.

'I won't really end up in Care, will I?' he said to Nadia, forgetting that he wasn't supposed to have heard.

She bent down and gave him a hug, smelling of hot washing-up liquid and splashing water down his neck. 'Course you won't, daft. I'll make sure you don't.'

Nathan felt reassured. She was a coper, Nadia. She'd coped all right with having a baby, setting

herself up in a council flat, getting a child-minder so
that she could go back to work at the supermarket. It
wasn't till after the baby was born that she'd met
Owen. She'd never let on who Katy's father was. He
was just someone who'd been and gone. Owen was
someone who stayed.

Once, Nathan had overheard the woman next door
telling the man in the newsagent's, 'It's the daughter
keeps that family together. Nadia. A good 'un, she is.'

And then she'd seen Nathan standing there with
the bar of fruit and nut he was waiting to pay for, and
she'd gone red and shut up. He wondered what other
gossip she'd been spreading. He didn't like the idea of
his family being talked about. It made him think that
if he did end up going into Care, people would cluck
their tongues and say, 'Well, I'm not surprised,' and
be pleased with themselves, for knowing what was
going on. Or what *wasn't* going on, more likely.

It was true that things would be far worse without
Nadia. Apart from coming round two or three times
a week and cheering things up, she made sure the bills
were paid, bought shopping and gave the place a
good hoovering every now and then. It was thanks to
Nadia that Nathan had gone on the Outdoor Pursuits
trip in Wales last term. She'd phoned the school and
found out about the Hardship Fund, and made sure
Nathan's name went down for an assisted place. It

had been great, that week, rock-climbing, canoeing, orienteering – it was the first holiday Nathan had had since Dad went, and the best one he could remember.

But Nadia had her own life, her own job. She was only twenty-one and anything might happen – she might decide to move away, travel abroad, anything. People did, at her age. Or she might get married, and go and live somewhere else – she had Owen, now. Owen *and* Katy – two massive slices of luck, as Nathan saw it. But they were a family on their own, the three of them. They didn't need Mum or Nathan. What would happen if they moved away?

Without Nadia, without Katy and Owen, home would be a dismal place. If it still *was* home.

He wasn't sure what it involved, being in Care. There used to be a house quite near the school, like a sort of boarding school, except that the children who lived there – six or seven of them – came to Hagley Hall. It had closed down now, because of Social Service cuts. Nathan didn't know where the children had been moved to. They wouldn't have any say in it, would they? They'd have to go wherever they were sent.

That could be him. He wondered what would happen if Mum got worse and worse, sitting there on the sofa while cobwebs formed around her and the dust settled. Like the crazy old woman in that book

Mr Barrington had read them bits of, *Great Expectations*. She'd given up living. But she hadn't died either, just sat there in her wedding dress, getting older and older. Perhaps that's what Mum was going to do, sit there while her eyes got more and more glazed, till she disappeared into her trance altogether.

'What's wrong with Mum?' he asked Nadia. 'Is she ill, or what?'

'Depressed,' Nadia said. 'It's a sort of illness, I s'pose. At least, there's things you can take for it. I've bought her vitamin pills and ginseng and stuff but I bet she forgets to take it. If only she'd go to the doctor. I expect she'll get over it sooner or later.'

But supposing she didn't? Supposing, Nathan thought, it wasn't something you could label as depression, something that could be cured by a doctor, or a phase she was going through? What if this was the way Mum *was*? What if she was going to be like this forever?

'Why don't you start on your homework while I cook this?' Nadia said, briskly chopping ham. 'I'll give you a hand with it if you like. If it's something I can understand.'

She was all right, Nadia.

Windfall

Afterwards, when he found out what it meant, he thought Windfall was a good name. Something that came your way by luck. An unexpected bonus.

It was.

After school on Tuesday (detentions at lunchtime and after school – Nadia's insistence that he did some work last night hadn't been enough to clear the backlog) he was at a loose end. Damien went for a swimming lesson, Smudge was at the market at Beckley, and Nadia wasn't coming round. Nathan could have got the bus to Beckley – Jo sometimes got that bus, if she hadn't got her bike with her – but instead he found himself thinking about that animal sanctuary. Dogs needing homes. He couldn't really have a dog, but he could go and look. He could pretend.

He knew where the place was and had seen it from the road. It was about a mile's walk from town, on a lane that gradually left the housing estates behind and rose uphill towards a Forestry Commission wood. There were one or two posh houses up here, behind thick hedges and big gates, and then there was Coldharbour Farm, with cows in the yard waiting for milking. Dogs barked as Nathan walked past the rutted farm track. Beyond it, set back from the road, was Windfall Cottage, large for a cottage but a rather dilapidated place with tiles missing from the porch roof, a tangle of honeysuckle almost obscuring the front windows, and washing draped over a spinner. A black-and-white cat sat washing itself by an open door. By the roadside, a peeling signboard read: WINDFALL ANIMAL SANCTUARY AND BOARDING KENNELS, and there was a proper entrance that by-passed the cottage and led to a collection of brick buildings, wooden sheds and animal runs.

Nathan hesitated. Now that he was here, he wasn't sure whether he could just walk in. There didn't seem to be anyone about, but he could see a dog – a red setter – standing on its hind legs against the wire of its run. There were chickens pecking about near the buildings; the grass was strewn with blobby white droppings and the odd russet or white feather.

Well, he could turn round and go home again, or he could go in. No one was going to tell him off just for looking, were they?

The newest of the buildings was a doghouse, with individual wire-meshed runs outside. Some of them looked empty, but he supposed the dogs could be sleeping inside. Each run had a litter tray, and bowls of water and food. The red setter bounded eagerly against the wire, and Nathan poked two fingers through to stroke its nose. That wasn't too clever a thing to do with a strange dog, he realised, but the setter was obviously friendly. It gave a whimper of pleasure and rubbed the side of its face against his fingers. Two runs down, a pair of fat Corgis waddled out to see what was going on.

'You want something?' a voice called out.

Nathan turned. The voice – not too friendly – belonged to a tall, skinny bloke of about twenty, dressed in black jeans and a white T-shirt with lettering across the chest. He was pushing a wheelbarrow loaded with dirty straw.

'I said, did you want something?' he said again. He had a thin face shadowed with stubble, and dark hair pulled back in a pony-tail. Nathan could only think that, whatever he'd expected the owner of Windfall Animal Sanctuary to look like, it wasn't like this.

'You got any dogs needing homes?' Nathan asked. Just for the moment, with his fingers still moist from the red setter's licking, he could pretend he was really going to get one.

The young man eyed him suspiciously. 'Yeah, there's a few. We don't give them away just like that, though. You'd need to get your parents to come up with you. You have to sign forms. And we do a home check.'

'OK,' Nathan mumbled. 'All that can wait, can't it? I just wanted to see if you'd got any, first.'

'Come on then. I'll show you.' The skinny bloke had dumped the wheelbarrow, and now he led the way towards another long shed. 'Those you were looking at are boarders. The ones for rehoming are in here.'

Nathan followed, uncertain. He heard barking – an eager, puppyish barking – from the shed they were approaching. This could be difficult. He'd see some fantastic dog, just the sort of dog he wanted, and then he'd have to go home and leave it here.

'What sort of dog did you have in mind?' the man asked. Nathan was close enough now to read the wording on his not-too-clean T-shirt. BUAV, it said. That was something to do with stopping experiments on animals, Nathan remembered. He'd signed a petition once, one of Jo's.

Nathan stared at him. This didn't seem the sort of place you could come to with special requirements: 'I want a pedigree Dalmatian,' that sort of thing. Surely you'd just have whatever there was.

'I mean, what sort of size?' the man explained patiently. 'Like, have you got a big garden? Are you going to be able to take it out for lots of walks? You've got to think about that sort of thing.'

'Oh, right. Yeah, lots of walks. But the garden's not very big.'

'Is there someone at home all day? We don't usually rehome dogs to people who are out at work full-time.'

'No, that's all right. My mum's there.'

God, he was getting in deeper and deeper. Any minute now, this bloke'd be arranging to come round to check things out at home.

They were in the shed now, in a sort of central aisle, with cages partitioned off on both sides, and hatches leading through to the outer fenced runs. 'There's this one, a nice little terrier,' the skinny bloke said. 'Only about three or four. Then there's a collie type, but probably a bit older than you'd want – need a lot of looking after, she would. Then –' he indicated the one that had been doing the puppyish barking, a poodle of some sort, not Nathan's type of dog at all '–this one's cute. If you like poodles.'

'I don't.' Nathan was going farther in, to see what dogs were in the remaining cages. In the next one on his left was a rough-coated mongrelly dog, long-legged, with ginger eyebrows. As soon as it saw him it ran to the back of its pen and cringed there, half-sitting, looking at Nathan fearfully. He could tell that it expected him to kick or strike out.

'I want this one,' Nathan said impulsively.

The skinny bloke caught him up and said, 'Sorry, mate. She's not one of the choices. She won't be ready for rehoming for a long time, if ever.'

'Why not?'

'Well, we don't know exactly what's happened to her, but she was found wandering about half-starved. From the way she behaves, I'd say she's been knocked about. She's terrified whenever anyone goes near her. Well, you can see. But you're all right here, aren't you, gorgeous?' he said to the dog, in a crooning, tender voice that surprised Nathan. She looked at him warily, her ears lifting, but didn't move from the back of her pen.

'She got a name?' Nathan asked.

'Hazel, we call her. We give them all names, even though they get new ones when they find homes. With her, she'll probably stay here and be Hazel.'

'Why can't she get a new home, when she's better?' Nathan asked.

'Too unpredictable. She can bite when she's frightened.' He showed Nathan his thumb, wrapped in dirty Elastoplast. 'That makes it very difficult to find the right home. Nowhere with young kids, for a start. And it's got to be with someone who'll take the trouble, who doesn't expect miracles. Someone who understands dogs.'

Nathan scuffed his trainer on the concrete floor of the shed. 'I could do that.' All at once, Hazel was exactly the dog he wanted. He even liked the name. She could have had some soppy name, like Brownie or Queenie or Susie, the sort of names people gave dogs. Or Elfie, like that stupid fluffy thing next door. Hazel was just right. Hazel. Nathan's dog.

The skinny bloke gave him a sideways look. 'Yeah, well, maybe you could, mate, but I told you – she's not available. You don't like the others?'

'Not as much as her,' Nathan mumbled.

'Why don't you come back in a week or two, with your mum and dad? There might be other dogs in then. And you could talk to the owner.'

'Oh – you ent the owner, then?'

The skinny bloke laughed, showing rather wolfish teeth. 'No, not me. I just work here. The name's Simon. Look, if you want, I'll write down your name and phone number. Then I can give you a ring if the right sort of dog comes in. You want something like Hazel, right?'

No, I want Hazel, Nathan thought. Now what? If he gave Simon his phone number, he'd be bound to ring when Mum was there.

'Come over to the office,' Simon was saying. 'There's paper and stuff in there.'

Nathan took a last look at Hazel and followed Simon out of the shed. 'The office' was a very grand name for what looked like some sort of bunker or bomb shelter – concrete, windowless, with just about room for a desk, chair and filing cabinet inside. A large sheep was taking an interest in the open doorway. Simon shoved the sheep aside, then went in and started burrowing about beneath files and heaps of paper, searching for a pen. It occurred to Nathan that he could easily run away, but for some reason he didn't. He stood outside the doorway of the office while Simon retrieved a chewed-looking biro from the muddle.

'What's your name, then?'

'It's Nathan. Nathan Fuller.' Why was he giving his real name? It would be so easy to make up a name and phone number. 'But look, I—'

'Yeah?' Simon looked up at him, pen poised on the back of an envelope.

Just then a girl appeared behind Nathan and spoke to Simon over his shoulder, making him jump.

'Jaz says it's all right for Saturday,' she said.

Nathan got a whiff of some sort of perfume she was wearing – musky, not the flowery stuff Mum wore when she could be bothered. She was standing so close that it would be rude to stare, but Nathan glanced sideways, getting an impression of long black hair, several silver necklaces, a purple T-shirt and a tattered black skirt whose tassels dangled over a pair of Doc Martens.

'Great,' Simon said. 'Have you told Ferdy and Erica?'

'Erica can't make it,' the girl said. 'Ferdy might be able to do a stint, though. We might just about manage.'

'We'll have to,' Simon said. 'This is Nathan. He's come about a dog. He likes Hazel but I'm taking his phone number in case something else comes in.'

'Hi, Nathan. My name's Saskia. She's lovely, isn't she?' The girl turned to look at Nathan. He almost clutched at the doorframe for support, because she was so amazing to look at. Her eyes were large and blue, ringed with dark make-up, and her gaze was very straight and direct. He stared back, fascinated.

'Anyway, Nathan Fuller.' Simon looked at what he'd written down. 'You were about to give me your phone number.'

'Er– well—' Nathan hesitated. For some reason, the girl's presence gave him courage. *Saskia!* He'd never heard the name before but it struck him as exotic, mysterious, just right. It suited her as well as Hazel suited Hazel. Perhaps she worked here too –

she looked too young to be the owner, only about seventeen or eighteen.

'Problem? Aren't you on the phone, or something?' she asked, still standing close to him, smiling encouragingly.

'Yeah. The problem is, I can't really have a dog.' He saw Simon staring at him, felt Saskia's gaze burning into his cheek, and plunged on, 'At least, I'd love to have a dog, I really want one, but we can't have one at home. My mum, she doesn't like dogs, doesn't like any animals. And we'd never pass the home check like you said. I just wanted to see what dogs were here. I was just pretending.'

'Oh, I see,' Saskia said, not at all shocked.

Simon put his pen down with only the slightest hint of exasperation. 'I thought there was something odd, to be honest.'

'So you're not allowed to have any animals of your own? That's tough,' Saskia said, and then, to Simon, 'Is it tea-break? I'm parched.'

'OK. Then I'll finish the calf house.' Simon looked at his watch. 'There's not much point waiting for Tessa and Malcolm. They might be ages yet. Like some tea?' he added to Nathan, to his surprise.

Saskia made tea from an electric kettle on a tray at the back of the office – climbing over stacked boxes to get at it – and Nathan sat in the doorway with his legs outside, occasionally warding off the curious sheep. He told Saskia and Simon about Prince, and about wanting another dog but never being allowed to have one. They didn't seem in any hurry to get rid of him, didn't mind that he'd wasted Simon's time and told lies. He made his tea last as long as he could, knowing that as soon as they went back to their work, he'd have to leave.

Before he'd finished, Simon stood up and said, 'Better get on. See you then, Nathan.'

That was it, then. He'd have to go. The intriguing glimpse he'd been given of Windfall, animals and humans, was all he was going to get. He stood up slowly, wondering whether to offer to wash up the tea mugs or empty Simon's wheelbarrow, just so that he could stay a bit longer.

'Tell you what,' Saskia said from her perch on the cardboard boxes at the back of the office. 'How would you like to help us out on Monday?'

'I've got school,' Nathan said, wondering if he could skive off.

'It's Bank Holiday, daft,' Saskia said, grinning. 'May Bank Holiday. Day off school – don't tell me you'd forgotten?'

'OK,' Nathan said promptly. 'I'll help.'

Simon laughed. 'Careful, mate. You don't know what you're letting yourself in for yet.'

Nathan wasn't worried. He'd have agreed to anything.

'We're going to the Show,' Saskia said. 'You know, the big show over at Hackleton? We're doing a stand, and we could do with a bit of help.'

'Doing what?' Nathan asked. 'It's all farmers and pigs and tractors, isn't it?'

'Yeah, and loads of people. Me and Simon are in an animal rights group, HAWC – Hagley Animal Welfare Campaigners, it stands for. We hand out leaflets and take money. You'd be amazed what people put in collecting boxes at shows like that. Give us a hand?'

'OK,' Nathan said again.

Soon after, he jogged home, happier than he'd been for weeks, with his head full of Saskia, Hazel, the odd place with its jumble of outbuildings and sheds and assorted animals. Only halfway back did it occur to him that he still hadn't met the owner of Windfall Animal Sanctuary.

The Side Entrance

Bank Holiday Monday, and Nathan was up early and off on Smudge's bike, anxious not to be late. He'd arranged to meet Simon and Saskia at nine. He cycled the five miles down country lanes, overtaken by lots of cars heading the same way, some towing horse trailers. As he puffed over the brow of the hill Nathan saw the whole showground ahead of him: a car-parking area, a main ring fenced off with white posts, several big marquees and whole avenues of trade stands.

It reminded Nathan of the time he and Smudge had gone to Brand's Hatch, just the two of them. It had been Smudge's idea, and Smudge had paid for the tickets – where the money came from, Nathan knew better than to ask. They'd left on Friday evening after school, not telling Mum; caught the coach to London then hitchhiked the rest of the way out into Kent, sleeping in a barn for a few hours in the early morning and having a breakfast of Coke and hotdogs once they got inside the racetrack. Nathan remembered how he'd felt that day: excited, not so much by the high-octane whine of the Formula One racing (though that had been great) but by the feeling that he and Smudge had got themselves right across London to get there, without adult help. It had almost been worth the trouble they faced when they got back home, very late on Saturday. Mum had been furious, though mainly with Smudge – Nathan was only thirteen at the time, and this was back in the days when Mum had been more like a normal mum. She'd given Smudge a real earbashing about leading Nathan astray, hitchhiking, and staying out overnight without a word about where they'd gone.

This was a different sort of show, but somehow the atmosphere was the same: car-loads of people, all with the intention of enjoying a good day out; the crackly lure of loudspeakers, promising excitement. The sun was already warm on Nathan's back, after early rain. He could almost smell the trees and the grass growing, all in lush early summer growth. It was going to be a good day.

He'd seen posters up at this time every year, advertising *Hackleton Heath Show and Country Fair,* but had never thought of coming. Country fair – if he'd wondered what it meant, he'd have pictured

Morris Dancing and maypoles. Saskia had explained that *country fair* meant things to do with killing animals – fox-hunting and shooting. There would be a parade of the Beckley foxhounds, and Saskia's friends planned to march into the ring as a protest. Nathan hoped he'd be allowed to join them.

'When you get to the gates, don't pay to get in,' Saskia had told him. 'Just say you're helping on our stall and they'll let you in free.'

But when he reached the entrance to the showground, the man selling tickets wasn't quite so obliging.

'Heard that one before,' he said, eyeing Nathan from under his tweed cap. Nathan knew what that look meant. It meant he saw Nathan as a teenage yob and possible juvenile delinquent. 'How do I know you're a helper? Get inside the gates and you'll be laughing. No, you can pay your four quid, same as everyone else.'

Nathan hadn't got four quid. '*Please* let me in,' he pleaded, trying to sound as polite and smarmy as he could. 'I *am* helping on a stand, honest. Got to be there for nine.'

'What's the name of it, then, this stand?' There was a show catalogue lying on the ledge of the ticket booth, and the man picked it up and ruffled through the pages at the back. 'It'll be listed in here, if you tell me the name. And you can't take that bike in. You can leave it in the car park.'

'The stall's called Animal – Animal— God, what was it? 'No, Hawk something. I can't remember.'

'Sorry, laddie. If that's the best you can do.' The man slapped down the catalogue. 'You pay up, or you clear off.'

Someone behind Nathan tutted, and he turned round to see a young father, next in the queue, with a twenty-pound note held out ready. Nathan considered making a grab for it, but instead he shouted, 'Tight, or what?' at the ticket man, yanked his bike round and cycled off. The people waiting behind him – all in an orderly queue, with money ready – stared at him, no doubt sharing the ticket man's view of him as a teenage vandal.

He didn't want to make trouble. He only wanted to get in.

Now what? He couldn't bear to let Simon and Saskia down, the first time they'd asked for his help.

There must be some other way. He cycled back to the lane, where a policeman was directing traffic, then turned right and cycled along the boundary of the showground. A mile or so farther along, passing a belt of woodland, fields and two farmhouses, he saw what he was looking for. A stile, and a green signpost labelled *Public Footpath*, pointing towards the showground across a field of yellow oilseed rape. There was even a convenient bit of scrubby wood, dense with undergrowth, next to the road. He hauled the bike in, hid it behind the rampant brambles, climbed the stile and set off across the field at a jog. The sickly sweet smell of oilseed rape tickled his nose, like overpowering perfume. He could see where he was going. Two fields farther on, and there was a stile into the showground, entering by the horsebox park.

The horse-boxes, densely ranked, formed a convenient screen. No one noticed him as he climbed the stile into the showground. Done it! So much for that ticket man with his 'Sorry, laddie' and his disapproving stare. Nathan tried to look as if he belonged here, and was on an errand for one of the horse-owners. He wasn't even late yet. Now all he had to do was find the stand.

Past the horse-box park was a sort of practice ring for the riders. Several show-jumpers were warming up their horses, cantering in slow circles, one rider putting his horse at a single high bar. Nathan stopped to watch, fascinated. They were enormous, these horses that the riders controlled with such ease. Their coats shone with grooming and their manes were plaited into tight knots. He stood by the ringside, smelling the sweat and the leather and the animal warmth, and felt dwarfed as the huge animals passed within feet of him, their hooves treading precisely in the rhythm of their cantering. One rider, a girl or young woman smaller than Nathan, hit her horse three times with the hefty stick she carried. The horse gave a small buck of annoyance and swished its tail, but carried on cantering obediently. Why did they put up with it, Nathan wondered, these powerful animals with twenty times the strength of their riders? Why did they tolerate the whips and the spurs and the bits in their mouths?

He could have watched for a long time, but he thought of the minutes passing and turned away from the horses into the main part of the showground. He saw show jumps, red-and-white poles, brush fences and white gates, and a horse cantering in to start its round. Most of the trade stands were grouped together in a long avenue leading away from the fenced ring where the main events took place. He wandered along, looking.

You could buy all sorts of things here, from tractors to toffee apples. The bigger, smarter stands were marquees, some with tables of drinks set out inside or even urns spilling over with flowers. It seemed an unlikely sort of place to find Saskia and Simon, among all these posh places selling conservatories or Land Rovers, waxed coats or all sorts of horsey stuff like saddles and rugs and boots.

However, as he wandered farther from the main ring, the atmosphere became less *Country Life* and more like an ordinary market, with stalls selling fluffy toys, candy floss and cheap jewellery.

He was going to be late after all if he didn't find them in a minute. He hadn't realised there'd be so many stands. Then he saw Saskia waving, from a small stand to his right. It was just one small tent, with trestle tables in front of it and boxes stacked behind. A banner draped across the front of the tables read HAGLEY ANIMAL WELFARE CAMPAIGNERS.

'You made it, then.' Saskia smiled at him in her way that made him feel special. She and Simon both wore white T-shirts printed HAWC below a picture of a hawk with wings outstretched. Saskia wore hers over some peculiar patchwork trousers in many shades of blue and purple, and a pair of dirty plimsolls. She wore purple eye make-up, that made her eyes look very blue against her raven-black hair. Nathan wondered whether her hair was dyed. Not many people had hair as black as that.

Nathan hadn't been able to resist telling Damien about Saskia. 'You should see this girl I met. Gorgeous, or what? And she liked me, I could tell.' He hadn't mentioned that Saskia was three or four years older than him and was probably Simon's girlfriend. He hadn't even mentioned Simon. Simon was all right, but Nathan was far more interested in Saskia.

'Hi, Nathan.' Simon was arranging leaflets on the table.

'I had a bit of trouble getting in,' Nathan said. 'That old bloke at the gate wouldn't believe me when I said I was helping.'

Saskia clapped a hand over her mouth. 'Oh no! I meant to leave a pass for you, but we were a bit late and I forgot all about it. No wonder you had trouble. God, I'm sorry, Nathan. Did you have to pay?'

'No,' Nathan said, rather proud of his initiative. 'I got in round the back, across the fields.'

He felt pleased that it was Saskia's fault rather than his own. Used to be being blamed for everything, he assumed that whatever went wrong must be his fault. But other people made mistakes too, and he didn't mind that it was Saskia, because it made her seem more like him, forgetting things. She had forgotten to leave him a pass, but she hadn't forgotten he was coming.

Now he had the whole day ahead of him. He looked at the leaflets and sales goods on display, wondering what he was supposed to do. The leaflets were all about different sorts of cruelty to animals – experiments, factory farming, trapping animals for their fur. And there were stacks of leaflets about fox-hunting.

'Who's looking after the animals today, then?' he asked, thinking of Hazel in her pen. 'Back at the Sanctuary?'

'Tessa. She's the owner. You'll probably meet her next time you come up,' Saskia said.

Nathan was so pleased that he couldn't think of anything to say. 'Next time you come up'. He was one of the team now. Even though he hadn't done a single thing yet, apart from turn up today. He wondered whether this Tessa had heard about him already. He pictured her as a horsey-looking woman with a weathered face, a no-nonsense sort of person – the sort of woman who'd normally disapprove of Nathan and assume he was up to no good. But she wouldn't mind him going to Windfall now that Saskia and Simon knew him.

'What do you want me to do?' he asked, indicating the trestle tables.

'Just let people help themselves to leaflets, and take money for the rest of the stuff,' Saskia said. 'Badges, T-shirts, car stickers – everything's priced. Sometimes people give donations. Here's the cash box.' She lifted out a tray of coins to show him. 'Notes go underneath.' The box already contained a twenty-pound note and a five-pound note as well as various sorts of change.

'What happens to the money?' Nathan asked.

'Does it go to the Sanctuary?'

'Sometimes,' Saskia said. 'But HAWC is a separate organisation. An animal rights group – we campaign and do stuff.' She waved a hand at the display. 'All this sort of thing. Petitions, protests. Sometimes direct action.'

'Yeah?' Nathan wasn't sure what *direct action* meant, but it sounded impressive.

'But today we've got to behave ourselves,' Simon said, glancing at Saskia. 'We're allowed to have our stall here on condition we don't disrupt their foxhound parade. 'Course, it *will* be disrupted, only they don't have to know it's anything to do with us.'

'Is it just the hounds that parade?' Nathan asked, wondering whether the dogs walked round the ring by themselves.

'No, it's the whole hunt – horses, the lot. The huntsman and the whippers-in all done up in their red coats,' Saskia explained. 'They bring the whole pack of hounds in and gallop round and the huntsman blows his horn, and the commentator says what jolly good fun fox-hunting is. It's a sort of advert.'

'What time's this happen?' Nathan asked, not wanting to miss it.

Saskia looked at her watch. 'First one in an hour, then another one this afternoon at three.' She had skinny arms and wrists, even skinnier than Simon's, and she wore an enormous green watch with a thick strap – Nathan was fascinated by every detail of her appearance. 'Only you don't know anything, right?'

'Right,' Nathan said, though he wasn't sure that he *did* know anything, or who he could possibly let on to even if he did.

It wasn't half past nine yet. This part of the showground was fairly quiet, and most people who came this way walked straight past the stand without even glancing at it.

'It'll get busier later,' Saskia told Nathan. 'Why don't you go and get us all a drink? Don't go to the van along there, it sells death-burgers. There's a health-food van further along.' She delved into a fabric bag for coins. 'Apple juice for me, tomato for Simon, and whatever you'd like.'

It was like being at the market with Smudge. Jingling the coins in his hand, Nathan walked along between the rows of stands. The avenue led back towards the main ring, through the bigger and smarter stands. To his left was a big marquee with a red car with L-plates parked in front of it, and a large signboard reading: ROADWISE DRIVING SCHOOL. LET OUR SKILLED INSTRUCTORS HELP YOU PASS FIRST TIME.

A man in a suit was standing inside the tent, talking to someone. Nathan stopped dead, his heart thumping.

Dad.

Promise

Someone bumped into him from behind, tutting. 'Stand right in the way, why don't you?' a sarcastic female voice said, close to his ear.

Nathan didn't answer. He didn't take his eyes off Dad. Dad was talking to the customer, a pretty young woman in jeans and a tight-fitting red top. He was laughing, smiling, making himself charming, the way Nathan knew he could.

Nathan didn't know whether he was churning inside or whether the whole world was reeling around him. Anger tightened his throat and tensed his neck; tears burned behind his eyes. Dad was here at Hackleton Heath, spending the whole day, probably, and hadn't even bothered to tell Nathan. Not knowing whether to walk on past, or confront Dad, Nathan stood there in a knot of indecision.

Dad hadn't noticed him. He made some joke, laughing at it. Then he took out a pocket notebook and wrote down details from the young woman. She smiled goodbye, flicked back her long hair and walked away, and Nathan saw Dad's eyes following her as she walked, her bottom swaying in tight jeans. Nathan hated her. He swallowed hard; anger was a rigid lump in his throat, ready to choke him.

'Dad!'

His voice came out all wrong, like someone yelling for help.

Dad's head swivelled round and his eyes focused on Nathan. He looked behind him to see if anyone had heard, then stepped forward, smiling.

'Nathe! What you doing here? Wouldn't have thought this was your sort of do.'

'I'm helping on a stall. With some friends.'

Friends came out defiantly. Friends, Nathan thought? Simon and Saskia? He hardly knew them, and they'd only asked him to come because they were stuck.

'Oh yeah? Going into Smudge's line of business, then?'

Dad stood in his smart suit, still smiling. His smile was stretched a bit too tightly. Nathan had never seen him in a suit until he started this driving school job. Underneath it he wore a crisp white shirt with a thin stripe, and a red tie. It made him look like a different person, someone who had nothing to do with Mum or Nathan or home.

'No. Not selling stuff. It's animals,' Nathan said. 'Leaflets about cruelty.'

Dad shrugged. Nathan knew that he'd never see the point of handing out leaflets, about cruelty or anything else. The world was the way it was. You made the best of it.

He clapped a hand on Nathan's shoulder in a matey way. 'Blimey, you've shot up, haven't you?' Their eyes were almost level. 'Be taller than me soon, the rate you're growing.'

'Why didn't you tell me you were coming?' Nathan said. The words burst out of him. He sounded like a little kid about to burst into tears.

Dad's smile wavered. 'How could I let you know? And anyway, I'm busy here.' There was no customer in sight, but Dad waved an arm as if to indicate queues of waiting clients.

'You haven't even phoned,' Nathan accused. 'You said you would, but you didn't. You don't—'

You don't care, he'd been going to say, but Dad made a shushing gesture with his hand, glancing over his shoulder. Nathan saw for the first time that there was another man in the tent, standing by a display screen. Another man with a smart haircut and suit, the same white striped shirt and red tie, like a clone of Dad but older and plumper. Nathan guessed that this was Dad's boss, who owned the driving school and had given Dad the job.

'Been busy, haven't I?' Dad said. 'Working overtime, weekends and that. You don't work regular hours, not at this game.'

'You don't work all the hours there are,' Nathan said, his voice hard and resentful. 'Not so's you couldn't even take two minutes off for a phone call.'

He was doing this all wrong. He remembered Mum saying once, after a row with Dad, 'Well, what d'you expect? Why'd he want to spend time with you, if you're such a long-faced misery?' But he didn't know how to make himself any different. He didn't know how to be the sort of son that Dad might want.

Dad smoothed his hair back. 'OK. Sorry. Didn't think this was your kind of show, that's all. Anyway, I'm going to be tied up all day.' He reached into his inside pocket, pulled out a wallet and took a ten-pound note from it. 'Here you are. You go off and enjoy yourself, right?' He held out the note to Nathan.

Nathan took it – after all, ten pounds was ten pounds – said 'Cheers,' and stuffed it in his pocket. He wasn't going to fall over himself being grateful. A ten-pound note wasn't the same as *time*.

'Tell you what,' Dad said soothingly, 'next Sunday, we'll have a day out together, shall we, you and me?'

'What'll we do?' Nathan asked, suspicious.

'I dunno. Whatever you want. We'll think of something.' Dad glanced back at his boss, who was looking into the distance with the sort of detached expression that meant he was probably listening in. 'Pick you up about – what, half-ten? At home?'

'You serious?'

'Course I am. I'll be there, promise. Look, I've got to get on. See you then. Next Sunday.' Dad had already half turned away.

For a few seconds Nathan couldn't think what he'd been doing before he saw Dad. Then his hand closed on the coins he was holding – warm and damp by now – and he remembered that he'd been on his way to get drinks, prune juice or whatever Saskia had said. Dad was already talking to his boss, their heads together, so that Nathan wondered if Dad was explaining who he was. Was Dad ashamed of him? Or perhaps he was lying, pretending Nathan was just someone he knew slightly. They didn't look much alike. Dad had the sort of stiff, wavy brushed-back hair that always stayed in place; Nathan's flopped over his eyes. Dad's eyes were blue; Nathan's were brown. Dad was quite stocky; Nathan was like a stick insect, Nadia said, with his sudden spurt of growth. He wished they were more similar, more like a father and son.

He walked on quickly so that he wouldn't seem to

be hanging around. He thought of Dad's smart new appearance – his hair cut short, his shirt white and crisply ironed. Who by? Who did Dad's ironing these days? Nathan couldn't imagine Dad doing it for himself.

Still, next Sunday. Nathan turned it over in his mind like an unexpected present he'd been given. Next Sunday, Dad was going to call for him and they'd have a whole day together. He'd try, he really would try, Nathan decided, to be happy and normal, not moody and sulky or a pain to be with. He'd make Dad want to be with him more often.

By now, Saskia probably thought he'd cleared off with the money she'd given him, and wasn't coming back. To make up for taking so long, he paid for the two health-food stall drinks out of Dad's ten-pound note, then went to an ordinary catering van to buy a Coke for himself. He deliberately took a different route back, going round behind the trade stands so as not to pass Dad again.

When he arrived at the HAWC stall, he found Simon and Saskia in the middle of an argument.

'But you *know* what we agreed—' Saskia was saying.

And Simon, stubbled chin jutting: 'Don't tell me what to do—'

Then, seeing Nathan, they both stopped talking at

once, leaving silence stretched in the air between them like a continuation of the conflict.

'Sorry,' Nathan mumbled. 'Met someone I know.'

Simon took his drink without saying thank you, gulped it down and walked off quickly in the direction of the main ring. Nathan looked at Saskia, who was wearing an over-bright, strained smile as she helped two little girls to find leaflets on pet care rather than the ones with pictures of rabbits having horrible things done to them in laboratories. Nathan knew that sort of look, all too well – it was the sort of look adults wore when they didn't want you to know they had problems of their own. Except that Saskia wasn't an adult, she was only about the same age as people in the sixth form.

When the little girls had gone, Nathan gave Saskia her money back, and she took it without noticing he hadn't spent any. She seemed distracted, looking at her watch every few moments.

He opened his can of Coke and Saskia turned round sharply, hearing the hiss. 'Coke!' she accused. 'Don't you realise what that does to your teeth, never mind your insides? And did you get it at the hamburger stall? They sell *dead animals* there.'

Nathan didn't like fruit juice but now he wished he'd bought himself something at the health-food stall. He should have known – Saskia and Simon were bound to be vegetarian. Now he didn't feel like drinking the Coke while Saskia was there.

'Nathan,' she said suddenly, 'you couldn't look after the stall on your own for half an hour or so, could you? It's nearly time for the hound parade and I want to join in the protest.'

'No problem,' Nathan said, and Saskia gave him her dazzling smile that made him think he'd do anything she asked. He wanted to see the hound parade himself, but they couldn't *all* go.

'Ta. See you later, then.' She threaded through the crowd, leaving Nathan to cope with a woman in riding clothes who snatched up one of the anti-hunting leaflets and waved it in his face.

'What right have you got to mislead people by handing out this sort of propaganda?' she demanded. 'Have you ever actually seen a fox hunt?'

'Course I have,' Nathan lied. 'Dozens of times.'

The woman looked at the other blood-sports leaflets on the table, turning each one over with the very tips of her fingers as though handling something infectious. 'It's disgusting, handing out this sort of thing.'

'Not as disgusting as doing it,' Nathan said. He felt rather pleased with that. He wished Saskia had been around to hear it.

Bundle

'Saw you at the show, yesterday,' Natalie Colburn said to Nathan in registration on Tuesday.

'Oh yeah?' He was trying to finish off his Maths homework before Mr O'Shaughnessy's lesson. He looked at Natalie guardedly from under his fringe. She was the sort of person who'd only bother to speak to you if she wanted to be snidey. 'What were you doing there?'

'Same as about three thousand other people. Walking round looking at things. Only me and Darren spent most of the afternoon in the beer tent, getting sloshed.' She giggled and looked towards Mr Kershaw in case he'd heard. 'More to the point, what were you doing there? I saw you at that animal loony stall. You're not into that sort of thing, are you?'

'What sort of thing?' Damien leaned over the desk, chewing.

If Natalie knew, then everyone would soon know.

'I was helping some friends,' Nathan said. 'Simon and Saskia.' He liked saying her name. Saskia. The way it hissed through his teeth, whispering itself into the air, mysterious.

'Oh, *Saskia*,' Natalie mocked. 'Sounds more like a dog's name. Saskia, the husky dog. Here, Saskia,' she called in a high-pitched voice, so that several people turned round to see who she was calling.

Nathan wished he hadn't given her the name to play around with, cheapening it. Natalie was like that. Now Damien was looking interested, and Nathan wished he hadn't mentioned Saskia at all.

'Saskia?' Damien asked, chewing with his mouth open. 'Is that the one you told me—'

'I work for them,' Nathan said, quickly improvising. 'Sometimes.' Well, it was true in a way.

'She's the girl who looks like something left over from the seventies?' Natalie asked. 'The one with the straggly black hair? Looks like a right slag.'

Nathan's quick temper betrayed him into flaring back. 'Who's talking? What d'you think *you* look like, with your skirt halfway up your bum?'

'Oo-*ooo*-ooh,' Natalie hooted, in her most annoying way. 'Fancy her, do you? Doesn't she go round with that long skinny bloke with a face like a wet weekend?'

'At least they *do* something. They didn't spend the

whole day hanging round the beer tent.'

'Natalie, come here,' Mr Kershaw called from the front of the class. 'And Nathan, I need to give you a new Blue Card. You'd better get your weekend homework out to show me.'

For once, bullied by Nadia yesterday, Nathan had done all of it except the Maths. Not very thoroughly, but enough to keep Mrs Reynolds off his back. Natalie ambled up to the front desk, and Nathan went back to his Maths, trying to finish it in time to show Mr Kershaw. But now Damien was interested in the weekend goings-on.

'So what happened then? At the show? You didn't tell me you were going. I'd have come too. I only went to watch Dad play cricket.'

'No, well...' It would have been altogether different if Damien had been there, Nathan thought. Damien wouldn't have wanted to spend all day on the stall, handing out leaflets, no matter how worthy the cause. They'd have walked all round the showground, then sat on the grass bank by the main ring eating burgers. That reminded him. He was going to ask Jo about being a vegetarian. He couldn't imagine Simon and Saskia being friends with him very long if he carried on eating dead animals. 'It wasn't very exciting,' he told Damien. 'Except the hound parade.'

'*Hound* parade? What, like a car rally, only dogs?'

'No, moron. Foxhounds. The Beckley Hunt. Horses and red coats and hunting horns and all that. Saskia and her mates did a protest, twice. The second one, in the afternoon, I went too. We marched into the ring with banners saying how cruel it is. So there's this snooty commentator saying what a great sport fox-hunting is, and how spiffing it is and jolly good fun and a great British tradition and all that guff, and there's us walking round with slogans saying *Ban it Now* and *Hounds off our Wildlife* and that sort of thing. Mine said *Stop Killing for Fun,*' Nathan said proudly. Saskia had told him that she and two friends had spent hours cutting up sheets and painting the slogans on Friday night. He would have helped if he'd known.

'And you were allowed to? Didn't the hunt people charge at you on their horses or set the hounds on you or anything? There could have been a right bundle,' Damien said hopefully.

'Well, there wasn't. The hunting lot just ignored us. We were allowed to walk round the whole ring once with the banners, and then these steward blokes in uniform came and shoved us out.'

Damien looked disappointed. 'So what's the point of it, then, if there wasn't a bundle?'

'The point of it, dummo, is to show the people

watching that hunting isn't just about smart red coats and nice horses. It's about tearing foxes to bits, for fun. Lots of them were clapping the hunt, but some of them clapped us, and cheered. I mean, they shouldn't be allowed to *get away* with it.' Nathan stabbed his pen viciously at his Maths book, piercing a blackened hole through the cover.

'I bet Mr O. makes you put a smart wallpaper cover on that, to cover it up,' Damien said. 'Are you *looking* for extra trouble?'

Nathan shrugged. He didn't have any smart wallpaper at home. Last time a teacher had made him cover an exercise book, he'd used a plastic carrier bag from Sainsbury's. Just then the bell went, signalling the end of registration, and he still hadn't quite finished the Maths homework. He'd really intended to do it this time, and would have done, too, if it hadn't been for Natalie and Damien rabbiting on. He thought perhaps he could finish off the last two equations at the start of the lesson, but Mr O'Shaughnessy, kestrel-eyed, saw him trying to do it under the table. Result: unpleasant words on his Blue Card, and a lunchtime detention. Great start to the week.

At the end of PE, the lesson before lunch, he remembered his detention and started walking slowly across the grass back to the main block and Mr

O'Shaughnessy's room, eating a Mars bar on his way. A flick of tail caught his eye and he saw a squirrel darting into one of the litter bins beside the concrete path. He stopped to watch it come out again. He quite often saw grey squirrels around the grounds; they lived in the trees by the old Hall, venturing out to forage for leftover food during lesson times. They probably lived on crisps and cheese sandwiches, Nathan thought. A quick, fluid movement, and the squirrel paused on the edge of the plastic bin, its tail fanning out like feathers. It was holding something in its mouth. Then it saw Nathan, hesitated, and ran away along the ground towards a big oak tree. Nathan expected it to run right up into the high branches – amazing the way they gripped the bark, even pausing on the way to look round – but instead it stopped in a low fork, sat up with its tail curled behind, and started to eat, holding the piece of food in its forepaws. Nathan gazed at it. He was close enough to see its cheeks bulging as it nibbled, and the paler fur of its underside.

Then there was a shout behind him.

'Watch me! I'll get it!'

It was Reado, with Eduardo and Jamie, coming from PE. Reado was running ahead, stealthily, low to the ground. He stooped and picked up a broken fragment of paving. Nathan glanced up and saw the squirrel still nibbling, taking no notice.

Nathan dumped his bag and lunged for Reado. Reado's arm was raised, holding the slab ready to aim.

'Put that down, you moron!' Nathan yelled.

Reado wriggled furiously. 'Get off me!'

'I said, put that down!' Nathan said, through gritted teeth.

Reado freed himself with a ducking twist, then straightened and shoved Nathan in the chest with his left arm. Nathan staggered backwards. Reado grinned and turned towards the tree, raising the slab again. Tensed with anger, Nathan rugby-tackled him, bringing them both heavily to the ground. Reado gave a yell of rage, kicking out and striking a glancing blow off Nathan's cheek. The slab was on the grass now – they both saw it at once. Nathan was quicker, stretching out a long arm and grabbing it. He raised himself high enough to hurl it away, in the opposite direction from the oak tree. Reado turned to him, his face screwed up with hate.

'What's got into you? You're mental – it's only a squirrel! My dad says they're just rats—'

'*You're* just a rat—'

They were both scrambling to their feet, squaring up, but then Nathan was knocked over by a sideways tackle as someone slammed into him. He lashed out blindly, and another pair of hands grabbed his collar, nearly throttling him. This wasn't fair – three on one! He staggered to his feet, wrenched his arm free and landed a satisfying punch on Reado's shoulder. Reado reeled back, and Nathan turned to confront the others. Little Jamie Day had backed off, but Eduardo was coming at him, grinning. Nathan raised his knee at just the right moment and Eduardo collapsed with a grunt. They'd been alone on the field when it started, but now children were coming over, little Year Sevens and Eights drawn by the excitement but taking care to stand well back, like an audience.

'*Fight! Fight! Fight!*' they chanted.

Reado grabbed Nathan from behind, arm bent round his throat in a choking grip. Nathan struggled and kicked, writhed free and then became aware that something had changed. The smaller kids were drawing back, no longer a jeering audience, but little groups of innocent bystanders.

'*You boys! Break it up!*'

Mr O'Shaughnessy was striding across the grass. Almost running, in fact. The boys broke apart, panting.

'What do you think you were doing?' Mr O'Shaughnessy demanded, glaring at each boy in turn. And then, as no one answered, 'I said, what do you think you were doing?'

What did he think they'd been doing? Discussing Pythagoras? Learning French irregular verbs? It was too obvious to need saying, but now Nathan found himself receiving the full whack of Mr O'Shaughnessy's outrage. 'Fuller! You're supposed to be in my classroom! Or had you conveniently forgotten?'

Nathan said nothing. He looked at the oak tree – the squirrel was long gone, up into the safety of the higher branches.

'Fuller started it, Sir,' Reado said, all contriteness and surprised innocence. 'He went mental.'

'All four of you, over to my office. Now,' Mr O'Shaughnessy ordered. 'Move, Fuller! At the double! I haven't got all lunchtime to spare.'

Nathan walked behind the other three, as slowly as he dared. Mr O'Shaughnessy was one of those teachers who turned sergeant-majorish when people played up. Most people – even Natalie – did exactly as they were told in his lessons; there was no messing about or answering back. Not that it was worth answering back, because he wasn't a great listener; he had no time for excuses. Nathan felt his face burning with the force of Reado's kick and his acute sense of the injustice of it all. He'd been on his *way* to Mr O'Shaughnessy's detention; he'd have been *on time* for once – what was he supposed to do, stand by while people stoned the school's wildlife out of the trees?

Mr O. had it in for him now, that was obvious. He made Nathan wait outside his office while he called in the others, one at a time. Nathan could hear fragments of conversation, Reado's high-pitched, wounded-innocent voice travelling through the door: 'He just went for me, Sir. He went loopy—'

He gave Nathan a smug grin as he came out. Nathan punched him on the arm and snarled, 'I'll get you, Reado!'

It was unfortunate that Mr O'Shaughnessy came to the door just in time to see and hear.

Inside the office, Nathan used his usual tactic of saying nothing, staring sulkily at the floor. He wasn't going to make excuses. What was the point, when Mr O'Shaughnessy wouldn't believe him anyway?

'...going from bad to worse...out of control... a danger to yourself and others...' Mr O'Shaughnessy's voice droned. 'And you're sullen, rude... I'm going to have to report this to Mrs Reynolds, of course, and I'm sure she'll be contacting your parents.'

Dismissed, Nathan used fine judgement in his closing of the door – certainly using more force than necessary, but not quite enough to be defined by Mr O'Shaughnessy as slamming. Outside the building, he felt anger rising again as he thought of Reado's smug face, the stone raised at the squirrel – Mr O'Shaughnessy hadn't even *considered* the fact that the fight had been three against one!

Nathan kicked a stone viciously, making it ricochet against the wall of the Maths office. Some Year Sevens scuttled hastily out of his way.

God, this place! Even when he *tried* to stay out of trouble, he couldn't. Two more lessons to get through, then he'd get another detention, at the very least, from Mrs Reynolds.

History and RE this afternoon.

No, thanks. He'd had enough of today.

Time to bunk off.

Hazel

'Oi, Nathe! Where you off to?' someone yelled as he jogged up towards the main gates.

He took no notice, hoping Mrs Reynolds wasn't around to overhear. Once through the gates he started running, his rucksack bouncing on his back. He ran till he was puffed out, then slowed, wondering what to do next, wondering whether it had been such a good idea after all. He'd only have to face more trouble tomorrow.

He had no idea where he was going until it suddenly came into his mind to go up to Windfall. Town was a bit dodgy during school hours. He'd truanted before and had felt himself followed everywhere by suspicious eyes; adults clearly felt that everyone under sixteen should be safely imprisoned in school for five full days a week. He loosened his tie and slipped it over his head, then pulled his shirt out of his trousers. With just a white shirt and dark trousers, he was unidentifiable as a Hagley Hall pupil.

He cut through the housing estates until he reached the end of Coldharbour Lane. The sun was warm as he walked, giving him a sense of freedom; this was like an unexpected holiday. The verges were thick with grasses and a cuckoo was calling from Windfall Wood, ahead of him. The woods and fields were so peaceful that he felt the last trace of anger fading. It was too good a day to spend at school.

If it hadn't been for Nadia turning up with Owen and Katy, bringing food to cook for lunch and insisting that they all ate together for once as a family, he'd have gone to Windfall on Sunday, the day before the show. He'd have spent the whole day there, if he could; Simon and Saskia had as good as said he could work there. And he wanted to see the dogs again, especially Hazel.

His brisk walk slowed as he reached the entrance. He stood by the signboard, looking towards the oddly-assorted buildings. Two chickens were pecking about on the grass and a goat lay in the shade of an apple tree. He might meet the owner this time; that could be tricky. She didn't know him, and might ask awkward questions about why he wasn't at school. He imagined her barking questions at him like a female version of Mr O'Shaughnessy.

Well, if he wanted to work here he'd have to meet her sooner or later. He hoped Saskia and Simon would be here, to do the talking for him.

He pushed open the gate and went in, greeted by a rising chorus of barks and howls from the row of kennels where he'd seen the red setter last time. Those kennels now had a different population – he saw a Border collie and a black Labrador among the inmates. Those dogs were the lucky ones, the ones with owners; they stayed a week or a fortnight and then went home. For Hazel, this *was* home.

As there was no one around, he thought he'd go and see her straight away, but then a small, fair-haired woman came round the corner of the kennel building. She was dressed in dirty jeans and a green sweatshirt with bits of stalks sticking to it, and she carried a big net of hay, slung over one shoulder.

'Hello? Yes?' She looked at Nathan as suspiciously as Simon had, last time.

'Is Simon here?' Nathan asked. 'Or—'

'Simon and Sue? Gone to the feed merchants.' The woman looked at her watch. 'They'll be a while yet. They've only just left.'

Sue?

'Saskia,' Nathan said. 'Is Saskia here?'

'Oh, right. I keep forgetting that's what she calls herself these days. She's Sue as far as I'm concerned.

Anyway, what did you want them for?'

Sue? Saskia couldn't possibly be called something as ordinary as Sue! Taken aback, Nathan stared at the woman, wondering whether this was Tessa, the owner. If so, she wasn't what he'd expected. She was younger, smaller, scruffier and altogether less formidable.

However, she gave him a straight look and said, 'Shouldn't you be at school?' and he realised that she was sharper than she looked.

'I'm on study leave,' Nathan said. Maybe she'd think he was old enough to be in Year Eleven.

'Shouldn't you be studying then?' She dumped the hay-net on the ground and pushed untidy fair hair out of her eyes. She couldn't be more than thirty or so, a good twenty years younger than the weatherbeaten *Country Life* woman he'd imagined. He should have known. *Country Life* women wouldn't be interested in looking after homeless and stray animals. They'd be too busy with their gun dogs and smart horses; too busy killing foxes and pheasants.

'I study at nights. And first thing in the morning,' Nathan improvised. 'You mustn't overdo it.'

The woman looked at her watch again. 'Well, if you want Simon and Sue, you'd better come back about six o'clock. I think they were going somewhere else after they'd picked up the feed.'

She bent to pick up the hay-net, turning away. To stop her, Nathan blurted out, 'They said I could work here. Help, anyway. I'm Nathan, Nathan Fuller.'

'Oh, did they? I think that's for me to decide.' She gave a tight smile that could have been amusement or annoyance. Then she gave him another of her straight looks. 'What makes you want to help out? Are you good with animals?'

'I dunno. I think so.'

'And you want to start today? Now?'

Nathan nodded.

'With your exams coming up?' the woman queried.

He shrugged. 'I'll fit them in all right.'

'Come on then.' The woman shouldered the hay-net. 'Let's see how keen you are. I'm Tessa, by the way. My husband's Malcolm. You'll probably see him around. If you stay, that is.'

Her tone made it clear that she would be the one doing the deciding. She glanced down at Nathan's school trousers. 'You'd better not wear those. It's dirty work. You'll smell like a muck heap when you've finished.'

'Don't mind,' Nathan said.

'Your mum might, though.' (*Some chance!* Nathan thought.) 'You'd better change. I'll fetch you some old clothes of Malcolm's – you're quite tall. Wait here a minute while I get them.' She dumped the hay-net outside a stable. 'You can have a look at Nightwalker – that's my horse. Careful he doesn't nip you.'

Left alone, Nathan looked over the half-door. The horse, plump and glossy black, was lying down inside, legs folded. He raised his head to look at Nathan, air fluttering through his nostrils in a silent whinny. Nathan wondered whether Tessa was going to tell him to clean out the stable, although the straw inside looked clean already. Horses were big, unpredictable animals, rather fearsome with their iron-shod hooves and sudden movements; he didn't fancy going inside a stable with one, especially one that might nip.

He glanced at the path Tessa had taken, round the back of the buildings towards the house. Then he looked in the other direction, at the open door to Hazel's kennel building. Furtively, he walked over and unlatched the wire mesh door. He went past the other kennels, though one of the dogs inside bounded up to him with a whine of pleasure. He went straight to Hazel's pen.

She was lying at the back, in exactly the same place she'd been lying last time. She cringed back as she saw him, sandy eyebrows lifting, ears flattening.

Nathan squatted by the wire door. 'Hazel! Come here. I won't hurt you!'

Slowly, her expression changed from fear to curiosity. With her eyes fixed on his face, she got up and crept towards him. He knew she would dart back if he made any sudden movement, so he kept quite still, calling her name softly. Gradually she came right up to him, and sniffed his fingers. Then she lay down, close to the wire, and he thought she relaxed. He was sure she recognised him from last time.

He didn't realise Tessa had come back until Hazel suddenly stiffened, looked towards the doorway, and ran to the back of her pen, tail low.

'Well,' Tessa said in a low voice. 'That *is* amazing. She's never got that close to anyone before.' She looked at Nathan curiously. 'All the same, you shouldn't take risks with strange dogs. How did you know she wouldn't snap at your fingers?'

Nathan shrugged. He just knew.

'And if you're going to help out here, you'd better get out of the habit of wandering around wherever you please,' Tessa said more sternly. 'We sometimes have sick animals in isolation. There's one now, a kitten.' She held out a bundle of clothes. 'Here. You can get changed in the office.'

Five minutes later Nathan was in a reeking chicken house, forking deep litter into a wheelbarrow. The stench nearly knocked him out, and the stuff was packed down hard, layer on layer of wood shavings and chicken shit. The sides of the roof pitched steeply, so that he couldn't stand upright except in the middle. Tessa obviously wanted to test his determination, giving him hard, smelly work. Well, he'd show her he wasn't going to be put off. Doggedly, he worked away, shovelling, scraping, going outside every now and then for a gulp of fresh air. Each barrowload had to be wheeled right round to the back of the farthest building and tipped on a manure heap. Tessa didn't come near him until he'd finished – cleared the lot, right down to bare concrete, and washed it all out and disinfected it.

Triumphant, he went to find her. She was in the office, writing something in a big ruled book. She came back with him to inspect his work. When she smiled he knew he'd passed, but she only said, 'Right. Now you can help me with the feeding. But I'll show you round, first.'

There were animal houses everywhere they could be fitted in – a stable for the horse, rows of pens for dogs and cats, the hen-houses, calf-boxes, hutches for guinea-pigs and rabbits, and an aviary of assorted birds. In a large cage by itself, at the back of the plot, there was a fox cub. It was curled up like a cat in the sunshine, opening its eyes warily as Tessa and Nathan approached. It was a lovely thing, Nathan thought, with its pointed face and russet fur that was still babyishly woolly.

'What'll happen to it?' he asked. 'Are you going to keep it?'

'No,' Tessa said. 'It'll be released into the wild when it's old enough. Its mother was run over, back in the spring, that's why it's here. No one's allowed to handle it, because we mustn't make a pet of it.'

Nathan thought of yesterday's hound parade. 'But supposing it gets killed by the hunt?'

Tessa shrugged, and said, 'That's the way it is for wild animals. They have to take their chances.'

She led the way into another separate building; a long shed called the Hospital House, whose present inmates were a swan with a damaged wing, the sick kitten and an ailing tortoise.

'Where do you get them all from?' Nathan asked.

'The animals? People buy dogs and then find they can't cope, or they dump them on the motorway. Sometimes they dump them on my doorstep. Sometimes people bring in strays they've found. Some are animals that have been shot at or snared. Some are cruelty cases, brought in by the animal welfare organisations. You'd be amazed,' Tessa said. 'I don't go looking for them, but they keep turning up. There's no end to the ways people can mistreat animals.' She said it without anger, as if stating a well-known fact. Nathan wondered how she could stay so calm.

'Hazel?' Nathan asked.

'She was found wandering around town, scavenging. The police dog handler had to catch her eventually, because the person who found her couldn't get near her. The owner's not been traced yet.'

Having assumed that Hazel was homeless, Nathan was dismayed by the mention of an owner. 'You mean she could be claimed? Even if she's been mistreated? Shouldn't the owner be fined or banned or something?'

Tessa nodded. 'Yes. They *ought* to be. Unfortunately the law doesn't work like that. You have to get a vet to say an animal's suffering before the RSPCA can prosecute. And with a dog like Hazel – well, she's a bit thin, but there's nothing else wrong with her. Nothing *physical*. Nothing you could prove. No, her owner's perfectly entitled to have her back, if he – or she – turns up and wants her.'

'But that's stupid! Why should people be allowed to have dogs if they're cruel to them?'

'Yes, I know. But that's what the law says.'

Tessa was leading the way back from the Hospital House, past a tatty caravan resting on breeze blocks near the orchard trees at the back of the plot. 'That's where Sue and Simon live,' Tessa explained.

Nathan looked. He still hadn't adjusted to the idea

that Saskia's name was really Sue, and the caravan took away his last hope that she might not be Simon's girlfriend. Half an hour ago this would have disappointed him, but now he was far more preoccupied with the idea that Hazel might have an owner. He was silent as he followed Tessa into the food store to prepare meals for the various creatures. All the foodstuffs were kept in a lean-to shed that backed on to the boarding kennel, with large bins containing calf nuts, oats, bran, chicken and rabbit food, and a table for cutting up the fruit and lettuce the tortoise required. All this food! Nathan's stomach was rumbling; he'd only had a Mars bar all day, and that seemed hours ago. He looked rather enviously as the full bowls were lined up. Tessa must have an amazing memory, he thought. She knew exactly what each animal needed to eat and drink, even remembering to add vitamin powders or medicines to some of the feeds. The whole business took nearly an hour, by the time Tessa had looked at various runny eyes, healing wounds and trailing feathers on the way round. Hazel, obviously hungry, didn't dare approach her food bowl until Tessa and Nathan had retreated to the door of the shed. Nathan wondered whether she'd have come if he'd been on his own. He knew he could win her confidence, if only Tessa would give him the chance.

'That's it for today,' Tessa said, when they'd finished washing up dozens of feed bowls at an old earthenware sink in the store. 'I've got one or two more animals indoors – besides my own cats and dogs – but I'll see to them in a minute, when I go in to cook. When do you want to come up again?'

Nathan thought about his week. Apart from school, there was nothing special until Sunday, and his outing with Dad.

'Tomorrow?' he suggested.

Tessa locked up the feed store and stood there jingling her keys. 'Don't forget your studying,' she said sternly. 'I don't want to be responsible for you failing your G.C.S.E.'s. Exams are important, you know.' Suddenly she was sounding like a form-teacher or Year Head.

'It'll be OK.' Nathan looked down at his feet. Tomorrow, or some time, he'd have to tell her that he wasn't really sixteen and on study leave. Then she'd be angry with him for lying.

'OK, then, see you tomorrow,' she said, smiling. 'You're all right. I get too many kids offering to help when all they want to do is stroke kittens and play with puppies. They don't want to get their hands dirty or push barrows about. But you don't mind hard work.'

Nathan walked home in a daze of pleasure. He

thought of the way Hazel had come up to him and sniffed his fingers. Tessa thought he was all right. He was going back tomorrow. He'd proved himself. Even clearing out the chicken shed, leaving it clean and smelling of disinfectant, had been rewarding in its own way.

Only when he got home did he remember that he'd truanted, and still had the consequences to face. And he was still wearing Malcolm's clothes.

Bother

Nathan walked slowly to the front door, wondering what to do about his school uniform. His tie was in his rucksack, and he could probably find another shirt, but he couldn't manage without his black trousers. Perhaps he ought to go straight back to Windfall, now, and collect them. But he was hungry – he needed something to eat first. There might be some bread in the bin. He'd make himself a sandwich and then go, on Smudge's bike.

He hoped Mum would be in her usual late-afternoon stupor and not even notice him, but no such luck. As soon as he let himself in, she was on her feet, yelling.

'Where've you been? I've had the school on the phone to me this afternoon, three times! You've been skiving, haven't you?' Her gaze fixed on the red-and-blue check shirt he was wearing, with Malcolm's denim jeans. 'And nicking stuff as well – you're the limit, you are!'

'I haven't been nicking!' Nathan yelled back. 'I've been working, if you want to know!' He looked around the room – at the closed curtains, the TV on as ever, the full ashtray and empty lager cans. 'You ought to try it – get off your backside for a change! Look at this place – it's a tip—'

'Working? Where? How much d'you get paid?'

Nathan pushed past her into the kitchen. 'I'm getting myself something to eat. If there *is* anything in this house—'

'You know there is. Nadia's been round.' Mum followed him. He reached out his hand for the fridge door but Mum darted in quickly, facing him. She was wearing the same sweatshirt she'd worn for the last fortnight, and her hair needed washing.

'Oh no,' she said. 'Not till you tell me where you've been. And why you've been skiving.'

Nathan turned away, urgent hunger fighting against his desire to keep Windfall a secret from Mum. She wouldn't understand.

'I'm going out, then. I'll buy myself something in town. Dad gave me some money,' he said nastily.

Mum stared at him. '*Dad?* When d'you see Dad?'

'Monday, at the show. He was there. At one of those stands. And he's taking me out on Sunday.' Nathan flung his words at Mum, wanting to hurt her with them.

Her eyes narrowed. 'You're lying. You're making it up. You've made some money today, or nicked it, and you're making up this story about Dad.'

'OK, have it your own way. But he's coming here on Sunday to pick me up.'

'Coming *here?*' Instinctively, Mum's hands went to her face, and smoothed over her hair. She was realising what a mess she looked, Nathan thought. As well she might.

'Don't worry,' he said. 'He didn't say anything about wanting to see *you*. I don't suppose he'll even come in. I wouldn't, if I didn't have to.'

Mum slumped away from the fridge and leaned against the doorframe. Her hurt expression surprised him. Usually, he could be as nasty as he liked – she hardly seemed to notice.

'OK, get yourself some food,' she said wearily. 'Or you can go along the road for fish and chips if you like.'

'All right.' He thought of hot salty chips, fish in batter, the tang of brown sauce. He was so ravenous that the thought almost made him drool. Back at Windfall, he'd been so hungry that he could have eaten the rabbit mix or the tortoise's lettuce.

'Only, Nathe – we've got to sort this out first.' Mum gave him a guarded look.

'Sort what out?'

'This truanting business. All this trouble at school. 'Cos you know what'll happen otherwise, don't you? We'll have social workers nosing round here, interfering.'

She didn't actually say *and you'll end up in Care*, but Nathan knew what she was getting at.

'Come and sit down a minute.' She went back into the lounge, and Nathan followed. The air was thick with cigarette smoke. Nathan pushed back the curtains and opened a window, coughing pointedly. Then he stood there, looking out. He and Mum never had cosy chats, sitting down together, and he wasn't going to start now. It wasn't her usual tactic. She must want something.

Mum didn't even turn off the TV, but instead of sitting down she went to the phone, dialled a number and waited. Then she asked for Mrs Briand, the Deputy Head. She pronounced it wrong: Briand, like Brian with a *d* on the end. Mrs Briand, who was French, pronounced her name *Bree*-on. 'Think of the cheese,' she'd explained, the only time she'd taken Nathan's class for a lesson, when one of their regular teachers was away. Nathan was alarmed to hear Mum asking for her. Usually it was Mrs Reynolds, the Year Head, who dealt with things like truancy and misbehaviour. Things must be getting really serious.

'Mrs Briand? Hello, it's Nina Fuller, Nathan's

mum.' She put on the fake posh voice she kept for people like Mrs Briand. 'Yes, he's turned up. Yes, he's fine. OK then, we'll see you tomorrow. Half past three, yes. Thanks a lot. Bye then.'

She put the phone down and stared at Nathan. 'See what you've done? See what a lot of worry you've caused? Nearly had the police out, she did. Now we've got to go to a meeting with her, after school tomorrow.'

'What for?' Nathan said sullenly.

'What d'you think? To sort out about you truanting. Fighting at school. All this trouble. You've got to start to behave properly, Nathan. I've just about had enough.'

'*You've* had enough? What do you ever do except mope about on the settee? You don't care where I've been! Mrs Briand cares more than you do! You wouldn't give a toss if she hadn't been on the phone!' To his horror, his eyes started to prickle with tears. He wasn't going to cry in front of Mum. He made his voice harden. 'When Dad comes on Sunday, I'm going to tell him I want to move in with him. I can't stand it in this pigsty.'

Mum had sat down in her usual place on the settee. She pulled a tissue out of her sleeve and started twisting it in her hands. It was disintegrating, bits of white stuff dropping on to the carpet. 'Go ahead. You tell him. See how far that gets you.'

Would Dad agree, if Nathan put it to him really tactfully? Stomping upstairs to his room, Nathan thought about how different things could be, with Dad. He'd never even been in Dad's flat, but he imagined himself living there, him and Dad, mates. Going out together on Saturdays, watching TV at nights, getting take-away pizzas.

Anything would be better than this.

There was a hard lump in his throat, getting in the way when he tried to swallow. He took off the borrowed clothes and put on his own jeans and sweatshirt, then slumped on his bed, staring at nothing, too miserable even to put on a CD. When he heard the front door open and Nadia's cheerful voice calling out, 'Hi Mum, Nathan!' he didn't even bother to go down. He heard voices downstairs: Mum's, Nadia's and Owen's. Nathan liked Owen, but he didn't feel like going down yet. He could hear Mum's voice raised and indignant, and knew she was telling Nadia about the truanting and the phone calls from school.

Soon he heard footsteps coming upstairs, and a knock on his door.

'Yeah,' he called out, expecting Nadia.

The door opened and Owen came in. Surprised, Nathan sat up. Owen had never come up here before.

He was twenty-one, the same as Nadia, tousle-haired and untidy, with big feet that tripped over things; his wide mouth stretched easily into a grin. To Nathan, he seemed permanently happy, liking everyone, expecting everyone to like him. Everyone did. Even here, with Mum the way she was, Owen managed to crack jokes and be cheerful.

'Mind if I come in?' Owen asked, already in, and closing the door behind him. 'Bit of bother at school, then?'

'Yeah. Wasn't even my fault.'

'Try telling that to a teacher. Believe me, mate, I know what it's like.' Owen sat down on Smudge's bed.

'You got in trouble at school, then?'

'Never out of it,' Owen said, picking up a cassette case. 'Not much good at school, me. Must have spent more time in detentions than I did in lessons. Sport, that was all right. But I hated sitting in a classroom. Left as soon as I could. Still, I regret it a bit, now. There's things I could have done with knowing.'

'What sort of things?'

'Oh, you know. If I'd got a few qualifications to my name I could have got a better job. It's all right being tea-boy at my age, but when I'm forty I'm going to look a bit sad, aren't I?'

'Is that all you do, make tea?' Nathan said. Owen

worked in an insurance office, but Nathan couldn't see how making tea was going to keep anyone busy full time.

'Tea, coffee. And I do the post. Hand out the mail, work the franking machine, go down the Post Office. Owen the Post, they call me, till it's tea-break, and then I'm Owen the Urn. A bit of photocopying, filing. All the dead simple jobs. Still, it's better than being on the dole and it keeps a roof over our heads. What you should do is, when some teacher gets up your nose, you should keep calm and say to yourself, I don't want to end up like that sad git Owen. I want a decent job.' He grinned, and reached into his pocket. 'Mind if I have a fag?' Pulling out a packet, he offered it to Nathan, who shook his head.

'I shouldn't really, only Nads won't have fag smoke near Katy,' Owen said, flicking the switch on his lighter. 'Does her nut if she sees me light up. She's got a point. I'm giving it up. In very gradual stages.'

'Here's Smudge's ashtray,' Nathan said, reaching round behind the curtain.

He lay down again and stared at the ceiling while Owen smoked. They didn't need to keep talking. Owen was easy like that; it was one of the things Nathan liked about him. Nathan wouldn't mind being like Owen; OK, the work sounded dreary, but Owen would never let that get him down. He'd go round joking with all the people he delivered mail and coffee to, and they'd all be fond of him and tease him back. Then there was the busking. Saturdays, that was what Owen did – sometimes in town, sometimes Oxford or Birmingham if he felt like a change. He was good. Nathan had seen him in town long before Nadia had even met him, doing a mime of a sad clown trying to give a bunch of flowers to someone. Owen had a proper clown costume that he'd bought somewhere and patched up, and huge shoes, and he painted his face with big sad eyes, and when he mimed he looked just like a clockwork model. Passers-by stopped to watch in fascination, and children asked their parents if he was really alive. 'You know that clown guy, the one that does the mime down the precinct on Saturdays? That's my sister's boyfriend,' Nathan had told Damien, proudly. Owen always referred to himself as thick, but Nathan knew he wasn't. A thick person wouldn't have the idea for that clown act, or the ability to charm an audience. Owen just hadn't been good at school; that wasn't the same as being stupid.

'Should have heard Nads just now,' Owen said after a while, breathing out smoke.

'What, is she mad at me?' Nathan said wearily. 'She hasn't even heard my version.'

'No! She's not mad at *you*. She was going on about

that Maths teacher, Mr O'Whatsit. He used to be *her* Maths teacher, she said. She's going up the school tomorrow with you and your mum, to sort him out.'

'Yeah?' Nathan tried to imagine it: the whole lot of them, sitting in Mrs Briand's office. He could imagine Nadia taking over, doing all the talking. Sticking up for him.

Really, he'd be far better off with Nadia as his mum.

'Come on then, let's go down.' Owen stubbed out his cigarette and swung his legs off the bed. 'Nads is cooking spaghetti. You know, her special way?'

Nathan thought of spicy sauce and the rich meaty tomato flavour. 'Yeah! Coming.'

Contract

Next morning – having dug out Smudge's ancient school trousers, which were on the short side but would have to do – Nathan carefully timed his arrival so that there wouldn't be time for anyone to ask him about yesterday. But Damien lurked in wait outside the mobile classroom, grinning and eager for gossip.

'Where did you get to, then?'

'Nowhere,' Nathan muttered.

'Great.' Damien made an exasperated face. 'I had to tell all sorts of lies about where you might be – course, that's what mates are for – and then you tell me you were nowhere. What d'you do, turn into the Invisible Man?'

'I was sick of O'Shaughnessy having a go at me,' Nathan conceded. 'Went up Windfall.'

'What, after that girl, the one you're always going on about? What's her name – Sisky, or Sukey, or something weird?'

'Saskia,' Nathan corrected. 'Anyway, I didn't see her. If you really want to know, I spent the afternoon shovelling chicken sh—'

'Oh, there you are, Nathan,' Mr Kershaw called from the doorway, holding the register. 'Thought I saw you coming. You're only just in time not to get a Late mark. And Damien, why aren't you inside? Mrs Briand wants to see you, now,' he told Nathan. 'You'd better go straight up to her office.'

'But I've got to see her later, after school,' Nathan protested.

'She wants to see you now,' Steve Kershaw repeated.

Damien raised his eyebrows and made a cut-throat gesture. Nathan walked up to the main building, pleased not to have to go into the form-room where Natalie and the others would be bound to gather like vultures. On the other hand, he'd got to face Mrs Briand now, on his own. Like the other Deputy and the Head himself, she was known to Nathan only through Assemblies and the occasional sighting round school. She had a posh office next to the Head's, in a part of the school Nathan visited only when he was in trouble.

He expected her to make him stand outside like a naughty boy, but instead her door was open and she called out, 'Nathan? Come on in.'

He hovered in the doorway, and she told him to sit

down. Then she got up and closed the door behind him. He could smell her perfume. She was quite old, with hair going grey, but she made herself look younger with suits and high heels, make-up and earrings. Nathan felt intimidated. He imagined Mum sitting here later on, with her tatty sweatshirt and lank hair. There could hardly be a bigger contrast.

'Well, Nathan,' Mrs Briand said. 'As you know, we're having a meeting later on, with your mother and Mrs Reynolds and Mr Hampshire, but I wanted to have a word with you on your own first.'

Christ! Mr Hampshire, the Head himself! Nathan didn't know whether to feel dismayed or flattered by the senior staff attention he was getting.

'You caused me a lot of trouble yesterday, you know,' Mrs Briand told him. 'I spent a long time making phone calls. I even drove into town to look for you.'

'I didn't go down the town,' Nathan mumbled.

'No? And you didn't go home. Where did you go?'

She was sitting quite close, trying to look straight into his face. Nathan stared at the carpet and shuffled his feet. He wasn't going to tell her about Windfall. She'd find a way to stop him going there, or she'd tell Mum, which would be just as bad.

'Just walked about,' he said.

'For four hours?'

He nodded.

'And what made you run away from school?'

He told her about the squirrel, the fight, the way Mr O'Shaughnessy hadn't even asked for his side of the story. Mrs Briand listened, but made no comment when he'd finished.

'Are things all right at home, Nathan?' she asked.

Nathan hesitated. She looked so sympathetic that for a second he felt tempted to tell her everything. But what would happen if he did? He'd be put in Care, and the family would be split up. He wasn't having that. When Mrs Briand met Nadia, later, she'd see that he had someone who cared about him.

'Yeah, fine,' he said.

When he got out of her office, he felt pleased with himself for seeing through her 'softly, softly' approach. That was the trick they did in police dramas on TV – the tough cop and the nice one. He'd had to promise to come back at break and lunchtime to sit in her office doing his homework, but at least that would keep him away from Damien and the others.

First lesson was History. Nathan arrived a little late, with a note from Mrs Briand to say he'd been with her. He showed it to the teacher.

'That's all right, Nathan,' Ms Hopcroft said.

He looked towards his usual place, next to Damien

at the back, but saw that Reado was sitting there. Ms Hopcroft pointed to the only empty seat, at the end of a row next to Jo, with Lynette the other side of her. He sat down there, and Jo smiled at him and moved her books along to make room.

Ms Hopcroft was new this term. They'd already had two other History teachers this year: Mr Wishart, who couldn't cope and had left; and then Miss Kelland, a temporary, who'd been fun but hadn't taught them much. Now, Ms Hopcroft. She was small and serious, with glasses and a pinched, earnest face. She had something wrong with one leg, and walked with a swing and a lurch, leaning on a stick. One of her shoes had a stacked-up sole. You wouldn't have expected it, but somehow she could keep order in the class, no problem. She had a withering line in sarcasm that could shut up even Natalie. She was a good teacher, too – so interested in whatever she was teaching that you couldn't help being interested too. The topic this term was Nazi Germany, and today they were learning about the persecution of the Jews.

It was at the end, outside the classroom, that the bad stuff started. Because of her stick, Ms Hopcroft always had to ask someone to carry her books and folders back to the History store-room after the lesson. Today she asked Lynette. Behind, the rest of the class spilled out into the corridor. Ms Hopcroft couldn't walk very fast, so there was a bottleneck. Reado, behind, started to mimic her lurching walk, pulling a moronic face. Some people started to laugh. As soon as Ms Hopcroft turned round to see what they were laughing at, Reado looked innocent; then, when she walked on, he started doing it again. At the store-room, Ms Hopcroft and Lynette turned left and went inside, and Reado lurched past them along the corridor. He mimed leaning on a stick, exaggerating the swing and tilt.

'I'm Miss Hopalong,' he lisped, screwing up his face. 'Miss Hopalong Cassidy.' A group of Year Tens coming the other way laughed at him. Acting up, he made his walk even more grotesque.

Then Jo pushed her way through, grabbing Reado by the arm and pulling him round to face her.

'Stop it! Stop it, you brainless nerd!'

Reado stared at her with his mouth open. 'What's got into you, birdbrain? I'm only messing about!'

'Messing about, you call that? Making fun of Ms Hopcroft, just because she walks with a limp? You're sick, you are! Sick and stupid! D'you want her to *see* you?'

Reado pulled a *she's dotty* face at his friends nearby. 'It's only a joke. Didn't know you were such a teacher's pet,' he mocked.

'I'm not anyone's pet,' Jo stormed back. 'I can't stand

that sort of thing. And you lot, encouraging him – you're just as bad. Picking on someone just 'cos they're a bit different – weren't you listening in the lesson just now?'

'Lesson? What's that got to do with it?' Reado was trying to walk along the corridor now, sensing that Jo was coming off best. You wouldn't want to tangle with Jo in determined mood, Nathan thought. She stood squarely in front of Reado, blocking his way.

'You haven't got a clue, have you?' she flared at him. 'Why don't you go ahead and call Lynette 'nigger' or 'wog', to see if she minds? It's the same sort of thing. What you call just messing about. You'd have been a good Nazi, no problem!'

The corridor was congested now. The Year Tens had pushed on past, but most of the Year Nines had gathered to see the outcome, and some smaller children were trying to push through, getting their bags wedged. Voices were raised, some in support of Jo, others jeering.

'All right, I said it was a joke! Don't get your knickers in a twist!' Reado yelled at her.

'My knickers are perfectly straight, thank you—'

And then a teacher's voice, cutting through the babble: 'Move along, you lot! Keep to the left!'

Reado took his chance to get away. Jo looked round for Lynette, who'd got stuck in the corridor traffic outside the History store-room; Nathan edged towards her.

'Good on you, Jo,' he said. 'Reado's a right idiot sometimes.'

'I hate that sort of thing! Reado thinks he's *so* clever – *so* funny – it's just pathetic!' Jo looked at Nathan so fiercely that he wondered whether she thought he'd been laughing. If he'd been a bit nearer he might have, till Jo waded in. When someone like Reado played the fool, it was easier to laugh than to stop and think.

'I wasn't laughing,' he said hastily.

'No, I know. You wouldn't. That's 'cos you're a human being with a brain,' Jo said.

Nathan, not altogether sure he deserved such a compliment, was about to say, *What, me?* But at that moment Mr O'Shaughnessy came down the corridor and gave him a suspicious look, obviously thinking that Nathan's mere presence meant trouble. Nathan stared back. This, at least, had been one bit of trouble he hadn't got involved in; though it might have been more to his credit if he had.

When Nathan went up to Mrs Briand's office at the end of school for the interview, he saw not only Mum and Nadia but also Owen and Katy waiting outside, sitting on chairs. Mum had made a bit of an effort,

brushing her hair and putting on earrings and a
cleanish T-shirt, and Nadia looked positively
formidable in a red jacket over her supermarket
uniform. Owen, holding Katy on his lap, grinned
sheepishly at Nathan – you might have thought *he*
was the one in trouble, Nathan thought. He'd
brushed his hair too, and even put on a tie. It was
bright yellow, and looked like an exclamation mark
against his navy-and-green checked shirt, but it was
still a tie.

Mrs Briand came along the corridor, smiling. Then
she hesitated, not sure whose hand to shake.

'So sorry to have kept you. Hello, Nathan. Mrs
Fuller?' She looked from Nadia to Mum and back
again.

'I'm Nathan's sister,' Nadia said. She stood up and
shook Mrs Briand's hand. 'I was a pupil here, before
you were Deputy. And this is Owen, and Katy, my
little girl. This is Mrs Fuller, Nathan's mum.'

'I see.' Mrs Briand, looking a bit taken aback by
the large turnout, shook hands with Mum, but not
with Owen, whose hands were full of Katy. 'Well, er,
Owen, would you like to wait outside with the baby
while we—'

'They're coming in too. Owen's family,' Nadia said
firmly, already on her way into the office.

'Well, I—' Mrs Briand seemed about to protest, but

then changed her mind and fetched in an extra chair. Owen sat on it, jiggling Katy on his knee, and Katy laughed and reached out a plump hand to clutch at Owen's hair. All right for Katy, Nathan thought. Owen was as good as a dad to her. He didn't care that her real dad was someone else.

'What a lovely baby,' Mrs Briand said, smiling at Katy.

'Oh yes, she's gorgeous,' Nadia said, smiling back, and then her face turned serious. 'About Nathan. He doesn't mean to get into trouble, do you, Nathan? And it's not always his fault. Like that fight the other day. Mr O'Shaughnessy didn't even bother to find out that Nathan was trying to save a squirrel. He just thought if there was a fight, it must be Nathan's fault.'

'We'll come to the fight later. There are a whole range of things we need to talk about, regarding Nathan's behaviour. As Nathan knows.' Mrs Briand looked round for Mum, who was sitting in the chair nearest the corner of the room, quite willing to let Nadia do all the talking. 'Mrs Fuller. As you're aware, Nathan truanted from school yesterday afternoon, and it wasn't the first time. Mrs Reynolds will be coming up in a moment and she can confirm how many absences he's had this year, usually unsupported by a note from home. And then there are the times he's registered with his form and truanted afterwards. I'm afraid the educational social worker will be getting involved if things don't improve. That will mean a home visit, and a careful monitoring of the situation.'

Katy let out a delighted shout, and Owen caught Nathan's eye and winked. Mrs Briand was looking at Mum for a response, but Nadia said quickly, 'He'll be at school all the time now, won't you, Nathan?'

Mrs Briand looked from Mum to Nadia, clearly puzzled about who was in charge of this family. Then she looked back at Mum. 'Mrs Fuller? You do understand how important it is for Nathan to attend regularly? Not just for his own sake, to prepare him for his exams, but as a legal requirement?'

Mum smiled vaguely and shrugged. 'I send him off to school in the mornings. If you can't keep him here, that's your problem.'

'Mum!' Nadia protested.

'I'm afraid it's your problem as well, Mrs Fuller. And Nathan's,' Mrs Briand said smoothly.

'He won't be—' Nadia began, but Mrs Briand was looking at Mum, who said, 'Well, I don't know what more I can do. I've told you enough times to stay out of trouble, haven't I, Nathan? You can't pretend I haven't. I mean,' she appealed to Mrs Briand, 'a lad his age, his size. What can I do?' She held both hands out pathetically. 'I send him off, like I said. I can't do more than that. Your teachers need to be a bit stricter with him, that's what.'

'Mum!' Nadia said again. 'How would that help?'

Nathan looked from one to the other. They were at cross purposes – Nadia trying to stick up for him, Mum blaming him. At least he wasn't having to say much himself.

'Between us, we must make sure that Nathan attends regularly, and stays at school once he's here,' Mrs Briand said. 'You haven't forgotten your SATS tests next week, have you, Nathan?'

'No,' Nathan lied.

'You may remember, there was a letter sent home about these tests – in English, Maths and Science,' Mrs Briand said to Mum. 'They're National Curriculum tests, sat by all fourteen-year-olds across the country, and externally marked. I do want Nathan to be here for these important tests.'

Mum looked completely blank, as Nathan knew she would, since the letter was screwed up in the bottom of his bag with several other forms and newsletters. The teachers were always going on about these tests, but Nathan hadn't paid enough attention to register that they were next week.

'I'm going to suggest three things,' Mrs Briand went on. 'One, is that I give Nathan permission to come up here at breaks and lunchtimes if he feels it will help him to stay out of trouble. And if he gets a detention from Mr O'Shaughnessy or any other teacher, he can bring the work up here. The second thing, Nathan, is that if you ever get to the stage where you think you're going to run away from school – and I hope you won't – I want you to come up here and tell me about it instead. And thirdly, when we've finished our conversation, I want Nathan to sign a contract agreeing to behave properly in school and to do the homework set.'

Mum nodded and looked satisfied. Well, she would, wouldn't she, Nathan thought – it must seem to her that Mrs Briand was taking over the responsibility. Nadia looked anxious, chewing her thumbnail.

'On your part, Mrs Fuller,' Mrs Briand went on, 'I must ask you to be meticulous in letting us know, by phone, if Nathan's genuinely absent for any reason. That will make it easier for us to follow up any – irregularity.'

That meant truancy. Nathan started to feel hemmed in by contracts and rules and agreements. Why hadn't he kept a lower profile? Now, he'd be watched wherever he went.

'Couldn't you tell Mr O'Shaughnessy to lay off him?' Nadia said. 'It's not all Nathan's fault, like I said. He doesn't mean to be difficult. He's a good boy really. It's not his fault he's moody sometimes. He's sensitive.' She looked at Nathan, who felt like a great idiot. 'It's just that things get too much for him sometimes, you know—'

Mrs Briand looked at her quizzically. Nadia stopped: on the brink, Nathan supposed, of saying, 'Things are difficult at home.' That was the last thing that needed saying.

'Yes, I'm well aware that Nathan isn't a malicious boy,' Mrs Briand said. 'You live in the family home, do you?' she asked Nadia.

Nadia hesitated, then said, 'No. I've got a flat in town, with Owen and Katy. But I go round at least three times a week.'

Nathan imagined teams of social workers poised to snatch him away from home the instant Mrs Briand picked up the phone. Between the two of them, Nadia and Mum, they'd get him into Care sooner or later.

'To go back to the truanting for a moment,' Mrs Briand said. 'I'm very concerned about Nathan wandering the streets during school hours. That's if you told me the truth, Nathan, about where you went yesterday afternoon?'

Nathan stared at his shoes. Then he blurted out: 'I didn't wander round the streets. I went up Windfall.'

Everyone looked blank.

'Windfall?' Mrs Briand asked.

'Windfall Animal Sanctuary. I work there.'

Mrs Briand was reaching for her notepad. 'Work there? How many hours a week?'

'You see,' Mum appealed to Mrs Briand, 'I can't get no sense out of him. He's never told me about this job.'

'It's not a proper job. I don't get paid. I help out.' God, why had he started? Mrs Briand was writing on her pad; next thing, she'd be on the phone, telling Tessa that he was in trouble at school and she'd better have nothing to do with him. He'd resisted Mrs B.'s attempts to get round him earlier, but now he'd given her another weapon to use against him.

'What do you do there?' Mrs Briand asked.

Nathan shrugged. 'Clean out cages. Feed the animals. Whatever.'

'He's always loved animals,' Nadia said.

Then Mrs Reynolds arrived, and she and Mrs Briand went into a two-pronged attack on Nathan: all about responsibility, respect for teachers, blah blah, until they were all ready to go into the Head's office. There, the Head looked at him sorrowfully and said how regrettable it was that things had reached this stage, and read out the terms of the contract. Nathan had to agree to do as he was told in lessons, to do his best to stay out of trouble, and to find Mrs Reynolds or Mrs Briand if he felt things were getting too difficult.

'Do you understand all that?' Mr Hampshire asked Nathan.

Of course he did. It was spelled out clearly enough for a baby of Katy's age.

'Yeah,' he said, and it came out on a rising note, sullen, and only just not rude. If this had been an ordinary lesson, he'd have barged out of the door, but he couldn't, with Mrs Briand in the way. He had no choice but to stand there feeling like a great dork. The only thing that made it bearable was catching Owen's eye. From Owen's expression, you'd have thought he was the one being humiliated. Then he gave Nathan the smallest of smiles, so slight that it was hardly more than a twitch of his mouth, but Nathan saw it all right and felt better. Owen knew what this felt like.

Mr Hampshire held out a posh silver Biro, and everyone watched while Nathan signed his name.

Don't Tell Simon

'Typical of you, that is,' Mum grumped at Nathan, as soon as they were out of the school's front door.

'What?'

'Clearing off to that animal place and never even telling me. You said something about working, but what use is that if they don't pay you? If you've got so much spare time you could spend it earning money for yourself, instead of scrounging off me.'

Nathan looked at her in disbelief. 'Great. Bloody great! Coming from someone who spends half her time loafing on the settee—'

'Come on. We're going to sort this out properly.' Nadia pushed herself in between him and Mum. 'There's no point shouting at each other. Why didn't you tell us about this job, Nathan?'

'Mum would have stopped me going,' Nathan mumbled. 'I like going there.'

'No, she wouldn't,' Nadia said.

'Don't see why they can't pay him,' Mum said. 'Sounds like exploitation to me. Next time you go there, Nathe, you tell them they can pay you, or you stop going. Why work for nothing?'

'Won't be going any more, will I?' Nathan said. 'Now that old Mrs Busybody knows about it. She'll be on the phone right this minute, saying I'm not allowed up there.'

'Don't be daft,' Owen said, pushing Katy in the buggy. 'She can't stop you doing things in your own time. She's not the Gestapo.'

'Might as well be.' Nathan scuffed his shoes on the pavement. With foreboding, he noticed a group of boys from his Year walking up from the tennis courts – no, not all boys, Jo was among them. The boys were Sanjay, Greg Batt and Eduardo. Of the four, three wouldn't gossip about seeing him come out of school with his entire family, but the fourth – Eduardo – would spread it all round the form before registration next morning. Damn. Nathan looked at his watch and saw that it was still only half past four; up there in Mrs Briand's office and the Head's, it felt like hours passing.

Nadia bent down to adjust Katy's bonnet so that the sun didn't shine in her face. Then she said, '*I* think it's a good idea for Nathan to work at this sanctuary place. Come on, Mum. He's always loved animals.

How about this – we say it's all right for Nathan to go up there, as long as he does his homework and stays out of trouble at school?'

'Well, all right,' Mum said grudgingly. Nathan couldn't see what difference it made to her, as long as he was out of her way.

'And I meant to tell you – there's a vacancy for a checkout assistant,' Nadia said, straightening up.

'Oh, come on,' Mum said, laughing. 'Checkout assistant? That means being smart and being polite to people. Can you see Nathan doing that, let alone turning up on time?'

'I don't mean for Nathan,' Nadia said. 'I mean for you.'

After school on Friday, Nathan went to Windfall.

He'd remembered to bring back the clothes he'd borrowed on Tuesday, to swap for his uniform trousers and shirt, and thanks to Nadia he even had a sandwich and a KitKat in his bag, but it would all be useless if Mrs Briand had been on the phone to Tessa and he was no longer welcome. He'd lied about his age; Tessa would know about that, too. He went into the yard, looking as usual along the row of dog pens to see what changes there had been. No one was around, so he went in to see Hazel. She was asleep in her basket at the back of the pen, dreaming. Her tawny eyebrows were moving and her front paws twitched. Nathan wondered what she was dreaming about.

He didn't want to wake her, so he wandered out into the sunlit yard and saw Saskia coming out of the feed store carrying two buckets.

'Oh, hi, Nathan.' She seemed pleased to see him, but then perhaps Tessa hadn't told her yet.

'Is Tessa about?' he asked.

'Taken Nightwalker out for a ride. Help me with the feeding? That'd be great. It takes ages on my own.'

'OK. I'll just change first.' Nathan went into Nightwalker's empty stable and put on his old clothes. When he came out, Saskia asked him to fill all the dogs' water bowls. 'Careful of the black mongrelly one in the end pen. He dashes out the door if you're not quick.'

'Right. Isn't Simon here either?' Nathan asked.

'Gone to collect a litter of kittens.' Saskia looked at her watch. 'He's only just left – he'll be a while, 'cos it's right out at Chipping Norton. Will you help me with something, after this? There should be time, if we get a move on.'

'Yeah, 'course.' Nathan looked at her, but she carried on scooping calf nuts out of the bin, saying no more. She was wearing a dirty white vest with her patchwork trousers and Doc Martens, and her hair was skewered up into an untidy knot, with bits trailing at the nape of her neck.

'Go on, then. Get on with it,' she said, turning to grin at him.

He almost blushed. He saw from the look on her face that she knew he'd been gazing at her. He couldn't help it; she fascinated him.

'I left Hazel's.' Saskia pointed to a tin bowl of meat and biscuit on the floor. 'I thought you'd like to give it to her.'

Nathan went straight to Hazel's pen. She was alert now and waiting by the wire, because the dog next to her was already gulping down its food. When he slid back the bolt on her pen, she growled and cringed automatically, then crept towards him, more interested in him than in the food. He let her sniff his fingers, put the bowl down and waited outside until she began to eat, very warily, making quick darts at her food bowl to snatch mouthfuls. Nathan would have stayed longer if Saskia hadn't told him to hurry. Following her instructions, he filled a hay-net and water-bucket for Nightrider, gave the rabbits some lettuce and pelleted food, and washed up dozens of dirty bowls.

'Right, that's that,' Saskia said, banging the bin lids shut. 'Now. I don't want you to tell Simon about this. Promise?'

'OK,' Nathan said, flattered.

'There's this donkey. We'll go and look at it now. In a field on the other side of the wood. I've seen it from the van a couple of times and I want to go over for a better look.'

'Is there something wrong with it?'

'Yeah, I think so. But I want to check. Come with me? We'll go the short cut, over the fields.'

'Shouldn't there be someone here?' Nathan asked.

'Yeah, officially. But the answering machine's on and we won't be long. If we don't go now, Tessa'll be back.'

There was a stile behind the caravan Saskia lived in, with a path leading to the orchard, another grass paddock beyond, and then out into fields of wheat. Across the valley, on the other side of a small wood, there was a red-tiled house in a cluster of trees – less than half a mile away but, Saskia explained, more than twice that distance if you went round by road. Following her along the narrow path through stands of green wheat, Nathan felt that his head would burst with elation and pride. Saskia had asked him to help her; she was sharing a secret with him.

'Why mustn't I tell Simon?' he asked.

'Well—' Saskia hesitated, then stopped and turned to face him. 'We don't always agree about how to do things. The thing is, Tessa lets us live here as long as we don't get in trouble with the police.'

'What sort of trouble? Have you been in trouble before?'

'Oh, loads of times.' Saskia carried on walking. 'Animal rights things. You know. Protests. Blocking the road outside abattoirs to stop the lorries getting in. Spraying slogans on butchers' windows. Causing a breach of the peace. We've both been cautioned, Simon as well as me, but now he's keeping his head down. He wants to start a university course next year, and it won't help if he gets a criminal record.'

'Have *you* got one?' Nathan asked, intrigued. All this made his own trouble at school seem tame.

'Not yet. Let's just say the police know who I am.' Saskia lowered her voice, though there was no one to hear. 'We had a bit of an argument at the Show on Monday, Simon and me. He thought it was enough to do the stall. I wanted to join in the protest. *And*–' she turned to Nathan with her dazzling smile '–let the tyres down on the Hunt lorries.'

'So did you?' Nathan asked, remembering the tension he'd noticed between them.

'Yeah.'

'Didn't you get caught? Wasn't it obvious who did it, with the stall there?'

'No. I don't suppose they found out till the end of the day, and by then we'd packed up. Anyway, there are plenty of people who hate blood-sports. Simon was furious, though, 'cos he said we won't be allowed to have our stall next year.'

They reached the small stream at the bottom of the field, and Saskia jumped across. Then she turned and went, 'Shhh!' to Nathan. 'I don't want anyone to see us here. Follow me.'

She went silently up the side of the next field, past a scrubby line of hedgerow. Nathan could see a gateway ahead, on their left, but Saskia didn't go that far. She stooped at a gap in the hedge. Nathan crouched beside her and they both looked through.

'There he is, poor thing. Look at his feet! I thought they looked bad when I saw him from the road.'

Nathan looked. The donkey was standing in a corner of the field, dozing. It was some distance away, but even so Nathan could see how poor its coat was, and then he noticed its hooves. They were so long that they curled up at the toes, like oriental slippers.

'Why's it got hooves like that? They look like horns, sheep's horns.'

''Cos his owner hasn't bothered to get the blacksmith. Their feet need trimming back, like horses' do. They grow like your fingernails would if you didn't cut them, only you don't have to walk on your fingernails. It's awful – it must be really difficult for him to move. And look at the grass in this field – all thin and thistly. There's hardly anything for him to eat.'

'What are you going to do?'

'Will you help me?' Saskia asked. Crouched together as they were, her eyes were very close to his. She gazed at him, pleading.

'Yeah! I said I would.'

'I'm going to steal him. Take him back to Windfall.'

'Now?'

'No. Someone'd see us on the road, and we can't take him back the footpath way because of the stiles. Early Sunday morning. It's the best time, with no one about. Simon always sleeps late, so I'm going to get up as soon as it's light, fetch the donkey and take him back to Windfall.'

'But then Simon'll know,' Nathan objected. 'And Tessa.'

Saskia shook her head. 'I won't tell them. I'm going to put him in the bottom paddock, past the trees. Tessa hardly ever goes down there – if she does, I'll say I bought the donkey at a market, or something. She doesn't have to know where he came from. At least I can get a blacksmith out to trim his feet. Will you be able to come, Sunday? Can you get up early?'

'Yeah,' Nathan said. He'd stay awake all night if necessary.

*

Back at Windfall, Saskia went to check the answering machine in the house, leaving Nathan outside. He went straight to Hazel's pen, opened the door and went in, crouching. Hazel was so nervous that anyone standing upright in her cage would seem threatening.

She was licking a front paw as he went in, but she stopped, laid her ears flat back and growled. Then he called her gently, and she pricked her ears and crept towards him. Talking all the time, he let her sniff his fingers, then moved his hand carefully round to the back of her neck, behind her ears. After he had stroked her for a few moments she came closer and laid her head on his knee. He was getting pins and needles and longed to straighten up, but he held his position to avoid frightening her. She would let him do anything now, he could tell. For some reason, she trusted him.

Then, just like last time, he became aware of Tessa standing in the doorway.

'You *are* making headway,' she said. As soon as she spoke, Hazel's ears went back and she slunk to the back of the pen, growling.

'She's all right with me,' Nathan said. 'Could I take her out, on a lead? She must be bored, shut up in here.'

'We might just try it,' Tessa said. 'She's getting

better every day, but she's certainly better with you than with anyone else. It's funny, that. Maybe there was a boy your size or smell, in the home she came from. A boy who was nice to her.'

Nathan didn't like to think of Hazel's home, a home she might go back to. Nor did he like the idea that he reminded her of some other boy. He wanted her to like him for himself.

'Nathan,' Tessa said. 'The first and most important rule here is that we don't get too fond of the animals. They come and go. They get new homes. You can try Hazel with a lead next time you come, but you must realise she won't be here for ever. Do you want to come and help me with Nightwalker? As soon as he's finished his feed I'm going to give him a good brush down.'

'OK.'

Reluctantly, Nathan left Hazel's pen and followed Tessa to the stable. He'd been so occupied with Hazel that only now did he realise Tessa wasn't angry with him – she hadn't called him a liar or a truant. That must mean Mrs Briand hadn't phoned after all. Yet.

Rescue

Smudge groaned and yawned as the alarm clock shrilled into the quiet of the bedroom. Nathan's hand lunged to grab and silence it. Typical! He'd assumed Smudge wouldn't be sleeping at home; certainly there had been no sign of him when Nathan went to bed, and Nathan hadn't woken later, as he often did, to find Smudge stumbling into the room, bringing beery smoky smells with him. It was just gone five, but already light; Nathan could hear birds singing outside. He'd have to get a move on to meet Saskia at half past. He'd set the clock for ten to five, forgetting its tendency to lose time.

'Oh, God.' Smudge screwed up his eyes, then pressed both hands against them. 'What the bloody 'ell you doing?'

'Go back to sleep,' Nathan whispered, getting out of bed and tangling his feet in Smudge's discarded jeans. 'It's early. And don't tell Mum I've gone out. I'll be back by about nine, right?'

Smudge made a *whurggg* sound and turned over, hunching himself under the duvet. Nathan found his own clothes and got dressed quickly, then went to the bathroom for a pee, not flushing the toilet in case it woke Mum. Her bedroom door was open – she only ever closed it if there was someone staying, like the loathsome Brian – and as he crossed the landing on his way to the stairs Nathan heard her steady breathing. She didn't usually appear till gone nine.

He put his key on its string round his neck and let himself out of the front door, then set off at a run. If Smudge's bike had been here he'd have taken that, but it wasn't in its usual place leaning against the side wall of the house; Smudge must have left it at Cheryl's.

It was nice being out so early on a summer morning, and he wondered why he hadn't done it before, just for the pleasure of being up before anyone else. The air was hazy, with the first pale sunlight touching the roofs. It would be hot later. The air was full of the song of unseen birds, and there was no one about – just a ginger cat that sprawled in the middle of the road and gazed at Nathan languidly as he passed. Then a white car turned the corner and Nathan saw its orange stripe. A police car...

He slowed to a walk, expecting a lowered window

and a stern voice: 'Where you off to, sonny?' But the police car was just cruising. As it passed he glimpsed the driver, and a WPC passenger who smiled at him, seeing nothing suspicious.

Walking quickly, he left the edge of town behind and walked up the lane to the Forestry Commission wood, where he'd arranged to meet Saskia at the picnic place. He couldn't meet her at Windfall, because all the dogs would bark and alert Tessa. He was a few minutes early after all, and sat on one of the wooden picnic tables to wait. Sunlight slanted through the edges of the wood, touching the grass with gold; he smelled the resin of pines. There were paths winding off among the trees, marked with symbols to show Forest Walks. If he had a dog – if he had Hazel – he'd come here every day. It was a great place for a dog, with acres of woodland to explore.

He thought of yesterday at Windfall, when he'd taken Hazel out on a lead. This time, when he approached her pen, she hadn't run back or cringed but had stood by the wire waiting for him. He had stroked her, and put on the collar and lead, and she hadn't minded at all. They'd walked all the way round the yard together. She kept close to his legs at first, her ears twitching nervously. Then, gradually, she began to look like a different dog – keen, alert, as if being with Nathan gave her confidence. Tessa was delighted: 'Well! Look at that! You've got a real way with animals,' she told him. Going home, he had felt a glow of pride. He wasn't used to being praised, and *this* – being good with animals – meant more to him than anything else.

After such a promising start, he wanted to take her out every day. On the days when he couldn't go, Tessa said that someone else would take her – Simon or Saskia, or Tessa herself. Jealously, he didn't want anyone else to go near her, although it was bound to happen, and better for Hazel that it did. But he would rather she cowered and cringed, even bit them. He knew this was an unreasonable thing to want, but he wanted her to stay as his special dog. If she let *anyone* handle her, she'd get a new home and be taken away. Nathan could hardly bear to think of that.

He heard the crunch of bike tyres on stones as Saskia rode in on the gravelled track.

'Great. You made it,' she said, panting a little.

'I said I would!'

Saskia looked as if she'd got out of bed five minutes ago. Her hair was tangled and her eyes were smudgy with yesterday's make-up, the way Mum's often were. 'I'll leave the bike here and collect it later.' She closed the lock and slipped its key into her pocket. She was dressed in an outsize black sweatshirt that Nathan had seen Simon wearing, and cut-off shorts.

Nathan couldn't help looking at her legs. Over her shoulder she carried a leather headcollar, for the donkey.

'Not half past yet,' Saskia said, pushing up her sleeve to look at her enormous watch. 'We'll be there before six. Come on. There's a footpath that leads out of the wood.'

They walked fast, sometimes breaking into a jog. Saskia wasn't as fit as Nathan, and he had to slow down to wait for her. He didn't want to get to the donkey field: he wanted to go on like this, walking in sunlight with Saskia beside him, pretending. He knew she had just got out of bed with Simon and he tried not to think of them doing sex, with heaves and grunts, the way he'd heard Mum with Brian behind the closed bedroom doors. He didn't really want Simon to get into his thoughts – he was in the way. Saskia and Simon didn't always get on well together, she'd told him that much, and anyway Simon was going away to university. Nathan imagined himself in some hazy future walking in the sunlit woods with Saskia, his girlfriend, and Hazel, his dog. He was already taller than Saskia and in a couple of years' time the age difference might not matter – anyway, she liked him, he was sure. They'd throw sticks for Hazel and he'd hold Saskia's hand, and then they'd sit down on one of the log seats and kiss and put their arms round each other, and Hazel would lie down to wait at their feet. When Simon was gone, there'd be a spare job at Windfall, a spare space in the caravan...

He tried to stop himself from thinking this, in case Saskia could tell. But he could think about it later.

The path left the forest trail abruptly and came out into open fields, cutting a line diagonally across a wheat field to join the path from Windfall they had taken on Friday evening. Nathan could already see the red-tiled cottage across the valley. Quickly, not talking, they made their way to the stream and up the side of the donkey's field. The dewy grass soaked Nathan's trainers and the bottoms of his jeans. A dog barked from the cottage and Saskia grabbed his sleeve and pulled him down behind the hedge, but the barking was half-hearted and soon stopped. The donkey was lying down by the field-edge nearest the house. Standing up again, Saskia produced wire-cutters from her shorts pocket, and wrenched at the tangle of barbed wire that held the gate shut. The gate creaked on rusty hinges as she and Nathan heaved it open, lifting it over the uneven ground. Then they were in the field, crossing the tussocky grass towards the donkey, who watched them with long ears held upright. Nathan hoped it wouldn't bray.

Saskia buckled on the headcollar and then gave the lead rope to Nathan.

'Come on. Up you get,' she said to the donkey, whacking it on the hindquarters. The donkey's ears went back, then it propped itself on stiff forelegs and lurched itself upright. Nathan pulled on the rope, but the donkey jibbed and pulled back.

'No, not like that,' Saskia said, taking the rope. 'Don't pull. Come on, walk,' she urged.

Stiffly, the donkey took two steps forward. Nathan could see how difficult it was for him to walk on those curled-up, untrimmed hooves. How on earth were they going to get him all the way round on the road? And the next bit was the most risky: they had to lead the donkey up the track, right past the cottage, and the dog would surely bark. Someone only had to pull back a curtain and they'd be seen.

Saskia made a clucking noise with her tongue, urging the donkey towards the gateway.

'Close it again,' she told Nathan, 'or they'll see straight away.'

She and the donkey made their agonisingly slow way through the gate and Nathan dragged it shut, trying not to let it creak too much. This was madness. Shouldn't they have muffled the donkey's hooves with sacking or something, the way he'd seen once in a film about smuggling? But even then, the donkey might bray. And Nathan remembered the police car. It only had to come cruising round the lanes, and they'd never be able to get the donkey out of sight in time. Two teenagers and a donkey, on the road at six o'clock in the morning – Nathan couldn't think of a convincing lie.

They were coming up alongside the cottage now, and he saw mown grass shining with dew, the white flowers of some climbing plant splashed against the wall, and well-tended flower borders. He felt a surge of anger at the people who lived there for looking after their garden but neglecting their donkey. The dog barked a few times, but no voice shouted at it to shut up, no curtain moved aside, and the most hazardous moment was past. They were on the road, on their way. But the donkey's walking pace was so slow that it would take a couple of hours, surely, to get back to Windfall. It moved its feet forward tentatively, like someone getting out of bed for the first time after a long illness, uncertain how to walk.

Saskia looked at her watch. 'We'll have to get a move on,' she whispered to Nathan. 'Here. You lead him.' She searched along the hedgerow for a chunky piece of twig, found one, and gave the donkey a hard whack on the rump. He laid his ears back and scuttled a few steps, then slowed again. Saskia hit him again, then came back to take the rope from Nathan. He was rather shocked by the strength of the blows she'd delivered, but understood why it was necessary.

'If only we could make him trot,' she said. 'But he can't, with feet like that.'

Slowly, with Nathan watching out for the police car round every bend in the road, they made their way back to Windfall. Nathan could have run the distance there and back four times over in the time it took, but at last they were outside the yard, and it was still only half past seven. No one was around, not even the chickens – a good sign, as it meant no one had yet come down to let them out of their hen-house.

The donkey's progress past the dog shed set up a chorus of barking, but before anyone appeared they were through the yard, past the small paddock where Nightwalker was turned out to graze, and into the lower field, screened from the house by a thick hedge. Saskia unfastened the headcollar and released the donkey into the paddock, where he started to tear at the grass hungrily. Nathan watched, relieved that the donkey's long, painful walk was over at last.

'There,' Saskia said. 'That's better grass than he's seen for a long while.'

'But what are we going to do about his feet? You can't sort it out yourself, can you?'

Saskia shook her head. 'No. I'll have to get the blacksmith out, some time when Tessa isn't around.

I'll work it out somehow.' Then she turned to Nathan and smiled. 'We ought to give him a name, oughtn't we? Now he's ours.'

Ours. Nathan liked the thought of that. Our donkey. The donkey we rescued together. He wasn't sure it was going to be as easy as that – surely the owners would report the donkey missing, or Tessa would find out? – but all the same it was a nice thing to think.

'I don't know.' He cast his mind around for a name, and then thought of the play he was supposed to be studying for his SATS test next week – *Twelfth Night*. His knowledge of the play was extremely vague; he knew there was a girl pretending to be a boy, and a bunch of people who got drunk and rowdy, but that was about all. However, there was one name in it he liked.

'Orsino,' he said. 'Let's call him Orsino.'

Saskia laughed. 'Orsino the donkey? Wouldn't it be better for Orsino the 'orse?'

'It's from Shakespeare,' Nathan explained. 'Someone in a play.'

'Oh, right.' Saskia thought for a moment. 'Yeah, *Twelfth Night*.'

'Did you do that at school, too?' Nathan couldn't imagine Saskia at school, in uniform.

'For GCSE,' Saskia said. 'OK, Orsino it is, then,'

she told the donkey, stroking his ear. She giggled, then, suddenly brisk: 'Come on, let's start doing the feeds. You've only just got here, remember.'

When they got back to the yard, Simon was in the feed shed, lining up bowls of various colours and sizes.

'Hi, Nathan,' he said, unsuspecting. 'You're early today. Are you going to take Hazel out later? Tessa said you were going to walk her again.'

Nathan clapped a hand over his mouth. 'God! I nearly forgot. I'm going out with my dad today. I'll do the feeds and then I'll have to push off home.'

Simon must think he was a right idiot, coming all the way here and then going straight back home. But he only laughed, opening a big tin of dog meat.

'Take the bike,' Saskia whispered to him outside; she slipped the key into his hand. 'I'll have to go back for it later, otherwise.'

Mum was shuffling about in her dressing-gown when he got back. She was in the kitchen, gazing hopelessly at the cluttered sink. Her hair was unbrushed and her feet were pushed into fluffy mule slippers of dirty pink. Nathan knew she'd forgotten too, or she'd have made a bit of an effort, for Dad.

She didn't ask where he'd been, but just said: 'Nathe, nip out to the shop, will you, for a couple of pints of milk? I'm dying for a coffee and the milkman's stopped delivering.'

That meant she hadn't paid the last bill yet. To keep her quiet, Nathan went to the paper shop for the milk, then went upstairs to shower and change. Smudge was still in bed, asleep with his mouth open, and Radio 1 on. Clean from the shower, Nathan searched for something to wear, found his best sweatshirt in a crumpled heap on the floor, and took one instead from Smudge's shelf. Then he combed his hair and glared at himself in the mirror. His face looked back at him, long and gloomy, with hair wet and slicked down. Damn – there was a spot coming, beside his mouth. He reached for Smudge's spot lotion and dabbed on an astringent dollop. He remembered that he was going to suggest moving in with Dad – that meant being the sort of son Dad might want to have permanently. He was going to be cheerful and witty and happy. He pulled at the front of his hair, wishing he could look more like Damien. Then he put on some of Smudge's hair gel and messed about with his fringe a bit more.

He intended to dash outside as soon as he saw Dad's car, but somehow he missed it. Dad was inside the front door talking to Mum before he realised. About to go down, Nathan heard them arguing, and drew back along the landing.

Dad's voice was disgusted. 'Christ, you're a state,

Neen. Ten o'clock and you're not even dressed. You're a wreck, woman.'

'So what? What's the rush?' Mum's voice was peevish, like a teenager's. 'What've I got to get up for?'

'This house is a bloody tip. Look at it. It's not fit for pigs to live in, let alone the kids.'

'If you care so much about the bloody kids, you could do a damn sight more for them,' Mum fired back.

'I'm taking Nathan out today, aren't I?' Dad said. 'That's why I'm here. Not for the pleasure of *your* company, I can tell you.'

'It's taken you long enough to give up your precious time for the poor kid—'

'Give it a rest, will you? I haven't come here for a row. Where is he?'

'Nathan? Aren't you ready yet?' Mum yelled up the stairs.

'Coming,' Nathan called miserably. Then he put on a cheerful smile, for Dad. Dad reached out and ruffled up his hair – so much for all that effort in front of the mirror – and said, 'Right, let's get going, then. See you later,' he said to Mum, with sarcastic pleasantness.

'Where are we going?' Nathan said, in the car.

Dad puffed out his cheeks, getting rid of any air

he'd breathed inside the house. Then he smiled, and said, 'There's a big funfair out Milton Keynes way. I thought we might check it out.'

A Day with Dad

Years ago, they went to Alton Towers, the whole family: Mum, Dad, Nadia, Smudge and Nathan, aged about eight. Nathan had spent the day in a bubble of excitement, rushing round, queuing for all the rides, not wanting to miss anything. He hadn't, not even the scariest rides that whirled him around and plunged him from dizzying heights and made him feel sick.

This funfair certainly wasn't Alton Towers but all the same he felt something of the same excitement now, as they parked the car in a grass field and walked towards the entrance. Dad was his, for a whole day! The air smelled of trodden grass and fried onions, and music thumped out from speakers. It was too early yet for the fair to be busy, and Nathan guessed that it wouldn't really get going until the evening. He could see only one or two people his own age; the fair's customers at present were mostly parents with small children. The rides were a bit tame: a big wheel, some attempts at white-knuckle rides, a ghost train and a house of horrors. It was quite an old-fashioned fair, with a shooting gallery where you could aim at a row of ducks moving along the back of a booth, and a hoop-la, and even stalls selling things like jam and tea cosies and plants in pots. Nathan wondered what he and Dad would do all day.

Wandering towards the big wheel, they passed a family with a young boy carrying a goldfish in a polythene bag. Nathan nudged Dad, who said, 'D'you want one? Shall we have a go?'

Nathan saw the sign, *Win a goldfish*, on the hoop-la stall ahead of them.

'No thanks,' he said. 'It's cruel, giving fish as prizes.'

All the same, he couldn't help going up for a look. To win a goldfish, you had to throw rings at skittles, and score with six out of ten throws. The stall consisted of a circular tent, with a man standing in the middle. Nathan saw a tank of fish on the ground, while some were in transparent bags hung up on the tent awnings, so that people could see what they'd win. The fish fanned out their delicate fins in the cramped space and nuzzled their mouths against the polythene walls.

'Want a go, mate?' the man at the stall asked Nathan. 'Pound for ten throws?'

'No, I don't,' Nathan said. 'What are people supposed to do with them? Carry them round all day? Then what – do you suppose everyone who wins one has got a tank set up at home, all ready?'

The man, who was about Dad's age and had a beer gut above sagging jeans, just shrugged. Dad was looking embarrassed, as if trying to pretend he had nothing to do with Nathan. Hanging back, he lit up a cigarette.

'It's cruel, giving animals as prizes,' Nathan insisted.

'Blimey, mate, they're only goldfish. If you don't want one, don't have one,' the man said, grinning. 'I've got other prizes as well.' He turned round and pointed to a row of small teddy bears with tartan bow ties. 'Have a go?' he appealed to Dad, who didn't answer.

'It shouldn't be allowed,' Nathan said.

The man stopped smiling. 'Yeah, well, it *is* allowed. So if you're not having a go, push off, OK?'

'Come on, Dad.' Nathan had a last look at the goldfish dangling in mid air, then walked off angrily, his hands pushed down into his jeans pockets. He turned to look at Dad, who was walking more slowly, smoking, looking amused.

'What's got into you?' Dad said. 'Like he said, they're only fish.'

'Fish are still animals,' Nathan said.

Dad laughed. 'Didn't know you were one of those animal rights fanatics. What's up with you – got a greenie girlfriend or something?'

'You don't have to be an animals rights fanatic to think that's cruel,' Nathan said angrily, ignoring the question about the girlfriend. 'How long are those fish going to last in plastic bags? I bet a lot of people get fed up with carrying them round, and throw them away. It's horrible!'

'OK,' Dad said, laughing again. 'It's not me you need to have a go at. I'm not giving the damned things away.'

Nathan didn't answer. He remembered his determination to be happy, good company for Dad. The day hadn't got off to a very good start. He couldn't stop thinking about those goldfish. If he had enough money he'd buy the whole lot, and take them to Windfall.

'Anyway,' Dad continued, 'you eat fish, don't you? Fish and chips, your favourite. What's the difference?'

'OK. Forget it,' Nathan muttered. It was true that he *did* like fish and chips, and he supposed he'd have to give that up too if he was going to be vegetarian, like Saskia. He still hadn't started. It wasn't very easy, at home. If there was a decent meal at all it was only because Nadia had made a special effort to bring stuff over and cook it, and it wouldn't be right to say he wouldn't eat this and wouldn't eat that.

They went on a couple of rides together – the big wheel and the ghost train, which wouldn't have scared a five-year-old, and then Dad had had enough. He steered Nathan towards a big tent that sold refreshments.

'You don't mind if I sit out the next couple, do you, Nathe?' he said, yawning. 'Had a bit of a night of it, to be honest. I'm feeling a bit the worse for wear – that big wheel's made me feel like throwing up. How about if I sit down here and have a coffee, and you come and find me after a bit?'

'OK,' Nathan said, disappointed.

This wasn't the sort of place to enjoy yourself alone. Why did it have to be *today* that Dad felt ill? Nathan wandered off disconsolately, went on another ride, more for Dad's sake than his own, and thought that it would be more fun if Damien was here with him. He began to feel a bit embarrassed. Suppose someone from school saw him, wandering around like a stray dog? He stood by a barrier, watching some young kids screaming with delight on the painted roundabout horses. There weren't any more rides he could go on without looking conspicuous among little kids with their mums and dads. Then he noticed two girls looking at him, giggling behind hands held up to their faces in the obvious way some girls had. They were only about eleven, and he couldn't tell if they fancied him or were making fun of him. They were much too young to bother with, but all the same he felt uncomfortable, unwilling to move away in case they thought they'd scared him off. He stared at the painted horses with their legs stretched out front and back as if in full gallop, unable to stop his cheeks from reddening. The girls soon got bored and drifted off, and Nathan stayed put, thinking that he could be with Hazel, taking her out on her lead, trying to get her to walk properly at heel and teaching her to sit. When no one was around he could have gone with Saskia down to Orsino's field to see how he was enjoying the grass. And there were the new kittens Simon had fetched on Friday, and Tessa had said someone was bringing some chickens in today that had escaped from slaughter when a broiler house had been cleared out. He'd rather be at Windfall. This was a waste of time.

He went back to find Dad, who was sitting in the beer tent with his *Sunday Sport* spread out on the table in front of him.

'Hi, Nathe,' Dad said, blowing out smoke. 'Enjoying yourself?'

'Yeah, great, thanks,' Nathan said. Whatever happened, he was going to stay cheerful, however difficult it proved to be cheerful with someone who wanted to sit and smoke and be quiet.

'Thought you'd have found someone your own age to hang around with,' Dad said.

Nathan shrugged. It sounded as if Dad wanted to get rid of him. Dad didn't understand. Nathan was fourteen, not a little kid at a nursery who could run off and find someone to play with.

'Do they sell Cokes here?' he said. 'I might as well go and get one.'

'Here.' Dad reached into his pocket. 'And get me another black coffee, will you? Two sugars.'

Nathan went up to the counter. A friendly woman in a blue overall got him the Coke and coffee, and when she handed him his change she said, 'A bit quiet at the moment, isn't it, love? You should have been here last night. Packed out, it was. Saturday night's when all the teenagers come.'

Typical. Wrong time, wrong day. Enjoying himself was hard work. Nathan carried the drinks over to Dad, who was engrossed in the sports pages and didn't look up for a few minutes. Then Dad yawned and rubbed his eyes, and said, 'Christ, I'm tired. Should have stayed in bed this morning. I feel like a dog's breakfast.'

'Where did you go, last night?' Nathan asked.

'Oh, just round someone's house. Few mates,

barrel of beer, couple of videos.' He winked at Nathan, man to man. Nathan tried not to resent the fact that Dad would rather have stayed in bed, that coming out today was a bit of a nuisance, that he was only feeling unwell today because he'd drunk too much last night. Nathan tried not to notice that Dad hadn't asked him anything about himself, or how things were at school or at home.

Then Dad yawned again, and said, 'This place isn't exactly Alton Towers. It's not as good as what I thought, to be honest, when I saw it from the road. Shall we call it a day – go back to the flat, pick up a take-away, see what's on the box?'

'OK.' Nathan was intrigued at the thought of seeing inside Dad's flat, which was in Beckley, the small town where Jo lived. Dad had been living there for about a year, but Nathan hadn't been round yet. Later, he thought, when Dad had revived a bit, he'd mention the idea of moving in. There was a school bus from Beckley, or he could borrow Smudge's bike and cycle in with Jo.

They finished their drinks and left, stopping at the burger place next to the supermarket outside Beckley to buy a take-away lunch.

'Burger and chips OK?' Dad asked, producing a twenty-pound note.

'OK.' Nathan noticed too late that there were

vegeburgers on the menu; he could have asked for one of those. But then Dad would have laughed and called him an animal rights fanatic.

Dad parked behind a row of shops in the High Street, then led the way through an alleyway to a door between the dry cleaner's and the office suppliers. There was a flight of steps that reached a landing and went on up to a second storey. Dad's flat was on the first floor, with another front door facing his.

'Here we are. It's not Buckingham Palace, but it's OK,' Dad said, opening the door.

Dad's flat was quite small and plainly decorated in shades of beige and cream, but everything looked clean, very different from the dirt and clutter of home. Nathan wondered whether Dad did the dusting and hoovering himself; it wasn't the sort of thing he could imagine Dad doing. There was a front room looking over the High Street, a small kitchen, and two bedrooms and a bathroom at the back. Two bedrooms! The spare one was used for junk at the moment, but Nathan immediately started to picture it as his own. Hazel could sleep in a basket at the foot of his bed. He looked out of the window at a walled garden below – just scrubby grass, nettles and a gnarled apple tree, and some old planks someone had dumped there – Hazel could have access to the garden during the daytime, while he was at school, and then he'd take her out for a walk as soon as he got home. He could help Dad out too – get the shopping, and take the rubbish down to the dustbin, and do some of the things Dad wouldn't have time for.

Dad was in the kitchen, getting out plates, knives and forks and tomato ketchup. They took their plates of food into the front room and sat down on the sofa to eat, while Dad turned on the TV and zapped from channel to channel. After the burgers, they ate ice-cream from the freezer and then Dad brought in some cans of lager and put on a video of a film he'd taped last night. It was a fast-paced American film, full of wailing sirens and car chases and shoot-outs, and muttered conversations in dark alleyways, and Nathan got a bit confused by the plot. When he turned to Dad to ask something, he saw that Dad was asleep, slumped back on the sofa with a can of lager in his hand. Soon he started to snore gently. Nathan concentrated on the film, so that he could tell Dad what was happening when he woke up. He finished off his lager, thinking of telling Damien about this: 'Went round Dad's. We watched a film and had a few beers.' It sounded a grown-up, matey sort of thing to do. Nathan wished he was enjoying it more.

Then someone rang the doorbell. Dad jerked awake, blinked at Nathan sleepily, then lurched to his feet and went to the door.

'Oh – hi,' Nathan heard Dad say. He laughed in an embarrassed sort of way. 'You've caught me having a bit of a nap. Good do last night, wasn't it?'

Nathan guessed it was a woman who had come to the door. He imagined Dad smoothing back his hair, trying to smarten himself up.

'I was just wondering whether you could spare five minutes to help me change a couple of plugs,' said a girly voice that sounded put-on. 'You know how helpless I am with anything like that.'

'Sure,' Dad said, sounding pleased. 'Thing is – I've got the boy here for the day. Nathan. I'll just tell him.'

Dad came back into the room, already looking far more wide-awake and cheerful than Nathan had seen him all day. 'Nathe, I'm just going upstairs to Kim's flat to help her out for a couple of ticks. You'll be OK, won't you?'

The woman had followed him in. 'Hi there. You don't mind if I have a lend of Barry for a little while, do you?'

'No,' Nathan said, though he did mind. The woman was a bit younger than Dad, with a round face and blonde hair in a frizz. Her feet were pinched into high-heeled shoes, and she wore tight jeans and a purple sweatshirt with a pattern over the front made of twinkling beads.

'Just tidy myself up a bit first,' Dad said. He went

into the bathroom, where Nathan heard him gargling. Kim giggled.

'Get on well with Barry, do you?' she asked Nathan, settling herself on the sofa.

'Yeah,' Nathan said, although he wasn't sure that was true. He and Dad had hardly said anything to each other so far.

'He's a good mate to me,' Kim said, looking sideways at Nathan. 'Always got the time to help me out when I'm stuck with something. All fingers and thumbs, I am, when it comes to plugs and wiring and things like that. Good bloke, Barry is. Bit of luck for me when he moved in here.'

Dad came back in, smelling of deodorant. 'Right then. You OK, Nathe? Help yourself to another beer. I won't be long.'

Nathan continued staring at the screen, though he'd lost track of the film completely. A few moments later he heard footsteps in the flat above, and voices, though he couldn't hear what they were saying. He kept thinking about what Dad had said: 'I've got the boy here'. He couldn't work out whether or not it had been said affectionately. Dad could have said 'my boy', or 'my son'.

He had a lot of time to think about it. The film finished, and Nathan took out the video and tried all the channels to see what was on, eventually settling for snooker, though he wasn't specially interested. He flicked through Dad's *Sunday Sport*. He drifted around the flat, wondering again what it would be like to live here. He got so bored that he thought of going along the street to where Jo lived; if she was in, they could go for a walk together, and he could tell her about Hazel. But he couldn't risk Dad coming back and finding him gone.

It was more than two hours later that Dad came back. By then Nathan was making a cup of tea in the kitchen; he hoped Dad wouldn't mind him helping himself.

'Sorry, mate. Took a bit longer than I thought. Got one for me?' Dad asked, noticing the tea. He looked pleased with himself. 'There's some biscuits in the cupboard. Hope you didn't mind me slipping out for a bit.'

'She must have had a lot of plugs that needed wiring,' Nathan said.

'Yeah, well, you know what women are like. They need a bloke around the place. She's all right, Kim.' Dad took a biscuit and held out the packet to Nathan. 'Look, mate, when we've had this I'd better run you back home, OK? I've got someone coming round later.'

Nathan stared. Already? Just when Dad was starting to feel better? And there hadn't even been time to tell Dad what things were like at home, or to test out how he'd feel about Nathan moving in.

'Poor old Nathe.' Dad ruffled up Nathan's hair. 'It's not been what we planned, really, has it? Tell you what.' He crunched another biscuit, and thought for a moment. 'I'm not working next Saturday or Sunday. How about we make a proper weekend of it? I collect you Saturday morning, you bring your stuff and stay over. We could even go up to Alton Towers if you like. That'd be better than that run-down do this morning, eh? And I bet they don't have goldfish for prizes there either.'

He grinned at Nathan, who smiled back. Next weekend! A whole weekend to look forward to! Today had been disappointing, he couldn't pretend it hadn't, but Dad obviously wanted to make it up to him.

At home, Dad dropped him outside. Nathan was relieved that he didn't come in to have another go at Mum.

'How was your day?' asked Owen, who was sitting on the lounge floor making a tower of plastic bricks for Katy.

'It was great, thanks,' Nathan said.

In the Donkey Field

Nadia was determined that Nathan wouldn't get into trouble this week. She made him do his homework, helped him to revise for the Science and English tests and got Owen to help him with the French vocabulary he had to learn. Then she checked his diary and made sure he'd got everything he needed in his bag for Monday, including a packed lunch.

'If you keep out of trouble all week, we'll go down the video shop on Friday night and you can choose whatever you like, OK? And I'll make you something really nice for your tea.'

With Nadia bossing him about, Nathan almost felt he could do it. The SATS tests were held in the main hall; there wouldn't be much chance to misbehave, even though he was bound to do badly. Especially in the second English one. That Shakespeare they'd been studying, *Twelfth Night* – with the lessons he'd missed for one reason or another, he'd never been able to get his head round who was in love with who, and who was pretending to be someone else. The bit he liked was about that bloke called Malvolio who was really big-headed and thought the lady Olivia was passionately in love with him. They'd spent a lesson acting out the bit where Malvolio had found the fake love-letter from Olivia. Greg Batt, surprisingly offering to play Malvolio, had been brilliantly funny. Nathan, who hated acting, had been forced to play Sir Toby, but it turned out to be fun. He'd be able to answer all right if they got a question about Malvolio. It was Olivia and Orsino and Viola and Sebastian that got him confused. And now, when he heard the name Orsino, he could only think of the donkey.

The Maths test was first. It was awful, sitting in the silent hall. Nathan hadn't realised how solemn it would be. He'd often seen the signs up, *Examination – Quiet Please*, in summer, and had glimpsed, through the hall windows, the older students working away at their exams for GCSE or A level. Now it was his turn to be imprisoned in there, with the whole of Year Nine. The desks were old-fashioned single-seaters, laid out in long rows, and six or seven teachers stood round the hall to make sure no one talked. Not that anyone would dare – even Reado limited himself to grinning at

Eduardo across the rows and mouthing something that Eduardo wisely ignored. It was so quiet that you could hear every sound outside – a bird singing, someone cutting grass with a strimmer, a lorry pulling up. Every time Nathan swallowed, he thought it echoed round the whole hall. Wherever he looked, he could see heads bent in concentration, fingers prodding calculator keys, hands writing. He felt panicky at first – no one could help him now – but he did what he could and then checked his answers, which Mr O'Shaughnessy had told them to do. Then he sat back on his chair and looked at the sunshine slanting into the hall, and felt quite happy. One test was over, and the science wasn't till Wednesday; he'd go to Windfall tonight and see Saskia and Hazel and Orsino, and on Friday Nadia would be pleased with him, and then there was the weekend with Dad. Things weren't so bad.

Leaving the exam, he caught up with Jo. He couldn't resist telling her, 'I've got my own dog now! Hazel, her name is. She's great.'

'Really?' Jo looked pleased. 'Did you get her from that sanctuary?'

'Yeah. I work there now. I'm the only one that can handle her,' Nathan boasted. 'She still lives there at the moment, but when I move in with my dad she'll come and live with us. He lives near you, did you know?'

'What, in Beckley?'

Nathan nodded. 'I'm going there this weekend. Staying with Dad.'

'Great! I hope it works out,' Jo said. 'Moving in, I mean. Come round if you've got time. We could take Hazel for a walk.'

'Yeah,' Nathan stalled, 'only I'm not sure what Dad's got planned.'

When they separated for their different lessons, he remembered that Jo had dad problems of her own; her parents were divorced, and for a while Jo had been staying with her mum and her dad on alternate weeks. She didn't seem to be doing that any more; she lived in Beckley in the flat above her Mum's health-food shop, with her mum and her nan. Nathan wasn't sure whether knowing about Jo's problems made him feel better or worse. OK, so he wasn't the only one whose parents couldn't sort themselves out. On the other hand, Jo coped with it much better than he did. *Jo* never had tantrums or stomped out of lessons or swore at teachers. If her parents' problems got to her, she never let it show.

At the end of the day, he went up to Windfall on Saskia's bike, which he'd brought to school. 'Where d'you get the bike?' Damien had said, waiting for Nathan in the driveway that morning. 'Oh, it's not mine, it's Saskia's,' Nathan replied airily. Damien raised his eyebrows quizzically, but Nathan said no more, preferring to let him speculate. Now, cycling up Coldharbour Lane in the heat of the afternoon and still in his optimistic mood, he found himself thinking about Jo and Saskia almost as if he could choose between them: they both liked him, he knew. He didn't chase girls the way Damien did – he wasn't confident enough and usually had too many other problems on his mind – and it came as a surprise now to realise that two such different and fanciable girls as Jo and Saskia were interested in him. Only in a friendly way, but still... It was nice to think of his donkey secret with Saskia, and going for a walk with Jo, and maybe, in the future, cycling to school with her. Then he remembered that Jo was leaving at the end of term, but even that couldn't dampen his spirits entirely. It would have to be Jo that was leaving, wouldn't it? Why couldn't it be obnoxious Natalie or snooty Judith or swotty Samantha, or, come to think of it, any other girl in the whole school? That time on the Outdoor Pursuits trip to Wales, he'd been in Jo's team for the orienteering exercise, and they'd got lost in the rain. That had been good, in spite of wandering about in the mist and coming last in the competition. Nathan had been the one who had realised how they'd gone wrong and how to get back to the Centre, and he knew Jo respected him for that. She and her mum were going to live in Yorkshire, Ilkley or somewhere – there were moors and hills up there, and she liked that sort of country.

Windfall looked deserted. It was so hot that all the chickens and ducks were lying under the shade of the bushes by the side of the gate, and only a desultory bark greeted Nathan's arrival. He parked the bike by the office and went as usual to see Hazel. She came straight to him, not cowering any more; her ears were pricked and she wriggled with pleasure at seeing him.

'You're my girl, aren't you, Hazel? My lovely girl.' He rubbed behind her ears and then she rolled over and he waggled one of her front paws. 'You can come and live with me, soon. I'll take you home. You're my dog now. No one's going to hurt you ever again.' He'd take her out for a walk once he'd changed his clothes, and seen Saskia or Tessa to find out what was going on.

He heard banging outside and went to see where it came from. Simon, crouched on the grass next to the caravan, was fiddling with some bits of wood and chicken wire. 'Hi,' he called. He didn't smile, or look particularly pleased to see Nathan.

'What you doing?' Nathan said, going over.

'Making a run. There are some new rabbits,' Simon said, not looking up.

'Want any help?'

'No, thanks,' Simon said curtly.

Nathan stood there undecided, wondering what he'd done wrong. Had Mrs Briand phoned after all? It was Tessa's reaction he'd been worried about; he wouldn't have thought Simon would be too bothered by school stuff. Simon looked like the sort of bloke who'd know for himself what it was like getting into trouble with teachers.

Then Simon stopped hammering, looked at him and said, 'If you're looking for Saskia, she's in the office.'

'Oh. Thanks.' Nathan didn't know how to take that. Why should Simon assume he was looking for Saskia? Did Simon *know*? Could he tell that Nathan wanted him out of the way? Nathan felt himself reddening.

'Look, mate,' Simon said, though not very matily, 'I know you mean well, but if you want to keep coming up here you're going to have to play straight. You're naive enough to let Saskia talk you into all sorts of things, and she will if you let her, I'm warning you. It was bloody stupid, stealing that donkey.'

'Oh.' Nathan's hands were sweating. He rubbed them on his school trousers. 'Well, it wasn't exactly *stealing*—'

'In law it was. D'you want to end up in trouble with the police?'

'No.'

'Well, that's what could easily happen. You can't go round helping yourself to other people's animals, whatever Saskia may have told you. And besides, there'd have been a chance of getting an RSPCA prosecution, if the donkey'd stayed where it was.'

'But the whole point was to get him away from there!' Nathan pointed out. 'Saskia wanted to get his feet done. The poor thing could hardly walk.'

'I know. But Saskia ought to know better. She should have phoned the RSPCA and got an inspector round to look at it in the field.' Simon rummaged in a tin for nails, matching the lengths. 'They'd have made sure the donkey's feet were done, but perhaps they could have prosecuted the owners as well. As it is, the blacksmith trimmed his feet today, so now there's no way of proving neglect even if we do get the RSPCA in. And the owners could simply deny it was their donkey, now he's here. It's only your word against theirs.' He untangled a length of chicken wire and stretched it against a wooden frame. 'Hold that for a minute, could you, while I bang in a couple of nails? So what I'm saying, Nathan, is think before you act, all right? If Saskia suggests any more mad ideas, I'd be careful before you agree, or else ask me or Tessa first. I know you *mean* well, but you could end up getting all of us into trouble.'

'But what's going to happen to the donkey now?' Nathan asked when Simon had finished hammering.

'You might well ask. Especially as Tessa doesn't know about him yet,' Simon said. 'So don't say anything, right?'

Well, obviously Nathan wouldn't, especially if it was going to get Saskia into trouble. He went to the office, and found her sitting on an oil-drum writing something in a large book at the desk.

'Hi,' she said, not looking up. Her hair was hanging in front of her face, and he wondered how she could see what she was writing. 'That poodle's been rehomed today. Great, isn't it?'

But she didn't sound at all happy, and when she pushed her hair aside and looked up at him he could see that she'd been crying. Her eyelids were reddened, with dark make-up smudged around them.

'Simon knows about Orsino,' she said bleakly. 'We've had a row about it.'

'Yes, he told me,' Nathan said. 'I mean that he knew, not about the row.'

'He thinks I'm a right idiot,' Saskia said. She leaned both elbows on the table and buried her face in her hands, and sniffed. Then she fished out a grubby tissue and said, 'Come on. Let's go and see him.'

'Simon?'

'Orsino, daft. Come on. He's had his feet done,

isn't that great? Tessa was going out to fetch some cats that had been found abandoned, and I phoned Jim – that's the blacksmith – and he said he could come in on his way to the riding school.'

She led the way over the stile beside the caravan and down to the second paddock. The donkey was grazing, his feet hidden in grass, and Nathan had to go close up before he could see that he had perfectly normal hooves now, trimmed into shape and neatly rasped.

'Isn't that better?' Saskia said proudly, leaning on Orsino's rump. 'Jim said he'll be tender on his feet till he gets used to it, but he can walk much more easily now.' Then she picked a stalk of grass and turned away from Nathan, and he saw her shoulders heave and realised that she was still crying.

'What's the matter?' he said uneasily. He wondered whether he should put an arm round her, comfort her. He would if he knew how.

Saskia sobbed for a few moments while Nathan stood there awkwardly. Then she recovered enough to say, 'It's Simon. We do nothing but fight, these days. Not just about the donkey. About everything.'

'What sort of things?'

'Everything.' Saskia blew her nose on the disintegrating tissue and sat down on the grass, facing the donkey. 'I mean, we used to do things together, protests and that. Now Simon criticises everything I do. Last week, for instance...'

Nathan sat next to her. 'What?'

Saskia sniffed. 'You'll think it's daft.'

'No, I won't. Go on.'

'Well, me and these mates, Erica and Ferdy – you know, the ones who were at the show – decided to do a demo outside the supermarket, about battery eggs. Ferdy's got this chicken costume – he dresses up as a huge hen, and we hand out leaflets to people going in, and tell them about battery cages and say if they're going to buy eggs, make sure they get free range. Well, we're only there about ten minutes before the manager comes out and says he'll get the police if we don't clear off. We had a bit of an argument about free speech and chicken's rights and this bloke says well don't go on at him, he doesn't decide what they sell in there, and besides they do have free range eggs so people can buy those if they want to. Anyway, eventually we gave in and went to the High Street instead. But when I told Simon about the barney at the supermarket he just said well what did we expect, if we hadn't got permission to be there? And he warned me again about getting a police record. Talk about yellow. I mean, you'd come with me on a demo like that, wouldn't you, if I asked?'

'Yeah,' Nathan said, though Mrs Briand rose up

inside his head like a Hallowe'en ghost, waving the contract he'd been forced to sign. It probably had a clause on it somewhere about not dressing up as a chicken.

His doubts must have shown in his voice, because Saskia turned to him and said angrily, 'That's how they get at you, you see. Be good, stay out of trouble, don't make a fuss, just let everyone go on buying meat and battery eggs and not having to think about the cruelty. That's how they've got to Simon. Be a good boy, don't get any black marks or you won't get the university place you want. It's not *fair*.' She hunched up her knees and wrapped her arms round them and bent her head so that her hair drooped over her face.

Daringly, Nathan reached out and touched her hair, stroked it. 'Don't cry, Saskia. It's all right. It's—'

Wrong thing to say.

'Don't be bloody stupid,' she said fiercely, jerking her head up. 'It's *not* all right and it'll never be all right till people start treating animals properly. People just don't care. That's what I can't stand! There's so much cruelty, everywhere, every day – chickens stuffed into batteries where they can hardly move, just so that eggs'll be cheap – strung up on production lines to have their throats cut, as soon as they stop laying – cows killed and burned because they've been fed the wrong food that gave them BSE – hundreds of thousands of healthy sheep massacred because we can't be bothered to vaccinate for foot and mouth – calves herded into pens at the market then taken away for slaughter – oh, it's too much – I just can't bear it!' She glared at Nathan. 'But what can one person *do*? I don't know about Simon but I can't just sit back and think about the nice clean police record I'm earning. I've got to do something!' She looked at him searchingly. 'You feel like that too, don't you?'

'Yeah, but—'

Nathan wasn't sure what to say. He'd never met anyone before who cared as passionately about things as Saskia did. He'd never thought about cruelty to animals on such an enormous scale, and when he did, he could only feel the same hopelessness as Saskia. What could you do about it? Food animals were just objects to be processed by a vast, uncaring system. It was easier to think about one mistreated dog, one neglected donkey.

'But what?' She was indignant again. 'Either you care, or you don't!'

'I *do* care. But – well, the police. I don't want a police record either,' he mumbled.

Saskia snatched at another stalk of grass. 'You're just like Simon. Goody Two Shoes. Keep your nose clean. I don't *care* if I get a police record. Even if it means Tessa throws me out. If I end up in prison I'll go on hunger strike.'

'And kill yourself? What good would that do?' Nathan retorted. 'D'you really think everyone in the world's going to stop eating meat, just 'cos you decide to starve yourself?'

'Oh, leave me alone.' Saskia scrambled to her feet, rubbing at her eyes. 'I might as well talk to Simon. I thought you under*stood*.' She turned, and started to walk back up the field.

'Wait!' he shouted.

'What for?' she flung back at him, but she stopped walking and turned.

He got slowly to his feet. 'If you were the one whose family was about to be split up, you might not want a police record either!'

Saskia stared. 'You kidding?'

'No, I'm not bloody kidding! I mean it. I don't want to get tangled with the police. Not 'cos I want to go to some poxy university, like Simon. It's because my family's in enough trouble already. If the police get involved, we'll be split up and I'll have to go into Care.'

'Oh, Christ.' Saskia's face softened, and her eyes filled with fresh tears. 'Why didn't you tell me? Why did you let me go on at you like that? I didn't mean what I said.' She came closer. 'You're all right, Nathan. More than all right.' Then she leaned towards him and kissed him on the cheek. 'Forgive me?'

'Yes,' Nathan mumbled, his face burning. Of course he did.

'Tell me all about it later. We'd better get back to the yard,' Saskia said, suddenly edgy. She glanced towards the edge of the upper field, where the caravan was. 'I don't want Tessa to come looking for us. We've been making enough noise, yelling at each other.'

Miss Mouth

Nathan did what he could of his English test, then sat staring out of the window into the sunlit morning, wishing he could be up at Windfall. He kept thinking about Saskia; he felt her kiss on his cheek like a badge of pride. Saskia! She'd actually kissed him! He probably could have kissed her back if he'd wanted to – if she hadn't rushed back up to the yard. Cycling back home yesterday, on her bike – she'd said he could hang on to it for a bit – he thought he'd tell Damien what had happened. But as soon as he got to school this morning and saw Damien waiting for him in the driveway, he knew he wouldn't. Damien would make it into a joke, make it crude.

Mr O'Shaughnessy was one of the teachers invigilating. Instead of just standing at the front or the back like most teachers did, he kept walking slowly up and down the rows, peering at people's work in an off-putting way. When he got to Nathan's desk, he glanced at the closed script, stared into Nathan's face and said, in a whisper loud enough to be heard by everyone in the hall, 'Why aren't you checking through your work, Fuller? Don't tell me your answers can't be improved on!'

'Done it,' Nathan mumbled.

Mr O'Shaughnessy gave him a disbelieving stare, then paced on up the row, looking more approvingly at the busily writing hands of the three people in front. Nathan thought of all those words being produced, everyone writing out what Mr Barrington had told them about *Twelfth Night* in class. They were like robots, programmed to go when you pressed a button. What was the point? It was like training a dog to do what it was told. Again, Nathan's thoughts drifted back to Windfall, and Hazel. His dog. She was getting so much better that she would walk with anyone now, at least with anyone she knew, but she liked Nathan best; even Simon acknowledged that. She was Nathan's dog. That was what he was good at – working with animals, not writing about poxy lovers and stupid plots. A way with animals, that was what he had, according to Tessa. Exams and Shakespeare weren't going to matter much. When he left school he could be a dog handler. What would it matter then whether Orsino loved Olivia or Viola?

When the exam was over, they had half an hour to spend in their History classroom before lunchtime. It wasn't a lesson: Ms Hopcroft was there to supervise, but she didn't expect them to do any work now that all the SATS tests were over. She told them that they could talk quietly among themselves, then sat at the front desk, marking essays. That was a joke – the idea of Year Nine talking quietly. Reado, for one, was incapable of speaking at anything lower than foghorn volume, and when he was together with a group of six other boys, including Damien and Eduardo, they all ended up trying to shout each other down. Their noise was rivalled from the other back corner by Natalie, Hayley and Lisa, while some of the quieter girls chatted quietly in pairs or took out homework or magazines; Jo and Lynette went round organising pairs for the inter-year tennis tournament. Ms Hopcroft could have kept them quiet if she'd wanted to, but she was busy talking to Samantha Warburton. Occasionally she called out, 'Keep the noise down, please, Year Nine,' but not as if she really meant it. Nathan sat on the edge of the Reado group, only half-listening. He was hungry, having had no breakfast, and he took surreptitious bites from one of the ham sandwiches Nadia had made for him.

'Miss, Nathan's eating,' Hayley shouted out from the back.

'Wait till lunchtime, Nathan,' Ms Hopcroft said mildly. 'It's only twenty minutes.'

Nathan slid the sandwich back into his lunch box.

'Oh, great,' Hayley huffed. '*I'd* get done for eating, but not him. Oh no. *Wait till lunchtime,*' she mimicked. 'Could you ever so nicely, Nathan, if it isn't too much to ask, Nathan, if you don't mind me asking, Nathan, stop stuffing your face?'

'Come on, Hayley, you know we all have to make allowances for *Nathan,*' Natalie said, with fake sweetness. 'Nathan's allowed to get away with anything, 'cos he lives in a tip and his mum's a slag.'

Damien had taken out his flashy new trainers to impress the other boys, but turned round to say sharply, 'Shut up, Natalie. Miss Mouth. Leave him alone.'

'Oh, poor little Nathan,' Natalie sneered. 'Needs you to stick up for him, does he?'

'Who are you calling a slag, anyway?' Damien retorted. 'We all know who the biggest slag around is. Someone not a million miles away from here. Someone who walks around with her skirt halfway up her bum. Someone who does it behind the bike-sheds every lunchtime with that spotty sixth-form nerd—'

'Oh yeah? Who you calling spotty, you creep?' Natalie flung at him. 'You're just jealous, that's all. I wouldn't go out with you if you were the only boy alive.'

Damien laughed, throwing his head back. 'Who's asking?'

'*You* did, after the Year Nine disco, remember?'

'You must have been drunk, Dame,' Nathan put in. 'Cross-eyed—'

Ms Hopcroft stood up and banged on the table with the board rubber. 'For goodness' sake! Is it too much to ask, that you spend a few minutes in civilised conversation? Do you have to resort to tribal warfare? Sit down, Natalie – no, in your seat, not on the desk. Damien, go back to your place. *Quiet* conversation, and I mean *quiet*, till the bell goes.'

Natalie sat down, but said to Hayley and Lisa, in a stage whisper intended to be overheard: 'Saw her on Sunday, with her boyfriend, didn't I? You should have seen them. Fat slag with dyed blonde hair. Great fat greasy bloke with a beer belly. Sitting in the pub garden, practically groping each other. Made me want to throw up.'

'*Who?*' Lisa whispered.

'Nathan's mum,' Natalie said, with a sidelong look at Nathan. 'And her bloke.'

Nathan heaved his rucksack off the floor, crashed it on the desk in front of him and stood up.

'Shut up, Natalie,' he said loudly. Then he hoisted

his rucksack on to his shoulder and marched towards the door, tripping over Eduardo's legs.

'Nathan, wait!' Ms Hopcroft said. Nathan ignored her. He got to the door and wrenched it open, then slammed it behind him. He had to get out of school, away from Natalie and her taunts, and go up to Windfall. The corridor was empty, but to get out he'd have to walk past several classrooms. While he hesitated, the door behind him opened, and Ms Hopcroft came out, leaning on her stick.

'Nathan!' she called, but he walked off quickly. He knew that was mean, because with her lurching gait she'd never be able to catch him up, but in his present mood he didn't care.

Then, just as he got to the library entrance, Mrs Briand came out.

'Hello, Nathan!' she said pleasantly. 'How did your exam go?'

'All right,' he mumbled, caught.

'Where are you off to now, then? Shouldn't you be in your lesson?'

'Just going to the library. Look something up,' he improvised.

'Good.' She stood aside to let him go in. 'Make sure you sign in with Mrs Abbot.'

And rather than stomping angrily out of school, Nathan found himself entering the hushed orderliness of the library, where a few sixth-form students sat working at tables or at the computers. Mrs Abbot looked up and smiled as he approached, and he said, 'Mrs Briand sent me in,' which was at least partially true. He signed his name, asked for the CD-ROM encyclopaedia, and sat down at one of the computers. If Mrs Briand hadn't been where she was, he'd be out of school, on his way to Windfall, breaking his contract. That would mean big trouble, risking visits from social workers and whatever would follow. All because of Natalie and her big mouth. There might still be trouble, if Ms Hopcroft chose to report him for walking out of her classroom, but he had the feeling she wouldn't. Anyone with half a brain would know that it had been Natalie's fault. Natalie and her big mouth… Aimlessly, he browsed the CD-ROM, not looking for anything in particular.

After about ten minutes the bell went for the end of morning lessons, and people started coming in. Amanda Flynn and Ellie Byrne, from Nathan's form, came in to return books, and drifted off to the fiction end of the library. After a few moments, to Nathan's surprise, Ellie came and sat beside him.

'Won't be long,' he said, thinking she wanted to use the CD-ROM. He'd go and look for Damien in a minute, eat the rest of his lunch, find out what had happened in the classroom after he left. Ellie watched the screen for a few minutes while he zapped from an article to a map and then a video frame, then he moved out of his seat and said, 'All yours.'

'I don't want the computer,' Ellie said, going a bit red. 'I wanted to say I don't blame you for walking out just now.'

'Oh. Thanks.'

'Natalie – she loves winding people up. I know what it's like,' Ellie said, looking at the table.

Nathan sat down again and removed the CD-ROM disc. Then he put it into its case to hand back to Mrs Abbot, and sat turning it in his hands, not knowing what to say. He'd been in the same form as Ellie for three years, but rarely spoke to her. She wasn't the sort of girl you'd notice in a group; she was quiet and always kept herself out of trouble. Her skin was flushed with embarrassment, and her blue-grey eyes darted shy looks at him.

'I think—' she began, and at the same time Nathan started to ask, 'What happened—'

'Go on,' she said, and Nathan said, 'No, you.'

Ellie flushed still more. 'I think you should try not to take any notice of her. She only does it because she knows you don't like it. If you could – well, I know it's hard – but if you could just laugh, even pretend you haven't heard, she'd stop doing it. It wouldn't be any fun.'

'Yeah.' Nathan scuffed the side of one shoe against the carpet. He always barged out first and thought about it afterwards, that was his trouble. He could think of the most marvellous things to say *later*, when he was in his next lesson or on his way out of the front gate, but at the time he just knotted up with anger and had to get out.

'I know it's not easy to do that,' Ellie went on, 'when she's just said something that makes you want to cry – at least, *I'd* want to cry – or hit her or something, but if you can, she'll get bored with you, and pick on someone else. That's what Jo told me, on the Outdoor Pursuits trip, and it worked. She hardly bothers with me or Amanda any more.'

'I didn't know you—' Nathan began, but at that point Damien's head poked over the screen that divided off the computer table from the rest of the library. Seeing Nathan and Ellie sitting together, he raised his eyebrows and gave a wolf-whistle.

'Well, well! Does the seductive Saskia know about this?' he asked Nathan.

Damn. Damien hardly ever came into the library. Ellie got up and fled back to Amanda and the safety of the fiction shelves.

'Thought you'd be miles away by now,' Damien remarked, grinning. 'Didn't know you had a secret assignation.'

'Didn't,' Nathan retorted. 'Come on, let's go out. I'm starving.'

He reached for his half-eaten sandwich as they went along the corridor, then saw Mrs Briand again, standing in the foyer with a coffee-mug in her hand, and he quickly put the sandwich away again until he got outside. Didn't she have anything to do, other than loiter in corridors? She nodded and smiled at Nathan and he smiled politely back.

If he saw Natalie, he'd kill her.

Great fat greasy bloke with a beer belly... He recognised that description all right. Natalie hadn't made it up about seeing Mum with a man in the pub. It was that slob Brian.

If Brian was back on the scene, Nathan was definitely moving out.

Phone Call

Hazel was learning fast. Nathan had taught her to sit when she was told, and was now teaching her *sit – stay*. He made her sit by the chicken house, then walked away from her across the yard to her run. Her eyes never left him, and once or twice she gave a small whine, but she sat where she had been told.

'She's intelligent, that dog,' Tessa said, coming out of the store-room with rubber gloves on. 'Very quick to learn.'

Nathan knew that. She was *his* dog, the best dog there was.

'Can you put her away now, and give me a hand?' Tessa said. 'I've got to clean and disinfect four of the dog cages – new boarders coming tomorrow.'

Nathan had hoped to show Saskia and Simon how well Hazel would sit and stay, but they'd gone to visit friends, Tessa said. He didn't dare go down to see Orsino, either, with Tessa around; she was obviously still unaware of the donkey's presence, or she'd have given him an earful and been a lot less friendly. When he'd helped with the pens and the feeding, he went back to Hazel to say goodbye.

'Not long now.' He pushed his fingers through the wire of her run. 'Won't see you tomorrow, but I'll sort things out with Dad, then you needn't be shut up in a cage any more.'

He rode home on Saskia's bike. She seemed in no hurry for it back, and he liked having it. He left it at the back of the house and went in through the open door. At first, from the smell of lemon-scented cleaner, he thought Nadia must be at home, but then Mum came in, smiling, with a sponge pad in one hand and a spray-can of furniture polish in the other.

'Hello, Nathe. Thought I heard you. Did you have a good time?'

'Yeah, thanks,' Nathan said.

He looked at Mum suspiciously. The radio was on and playing cheerful music, she'd brushed her hair and put on clothes that for once didn't look as if they'd been bundled up in a heap and kicked around the floor.

'What's all this for?' he asked, indicating the clean kitchen.

'Got to make a bit of an effort, haven't I?' Mum

said. 'You hungry? There's plenty in the fridge. Why don't you choose what you want and make a start while I finish the hoovering?'

Hoovering? Mum? At half past six on a Friday evening? He looked in the fridge, and saw packets of ready meals stacked up on one side, and a strawberry cheesecake in a box. He looked at the other items, and chose one that didn't have meat in it – cauliflower cheese. He was reading the instructions when Mum came back in.

'Not the cheesecake. That's for tomorrow.' She looked at the packet Nathan was holding. 'Do chips with that if you like. There's a packet in the freezer. We'll have ice-cream for afters.'

She picked up a wine-box from the floor, ripped open the packaging and stood it on one of the work surfaces, then fitted the tap attachment and filled a glass for herself. 'Cheers! There's Coke in the bottom of the fridge, or have a lager if you like.'

'You celebrating or something?' Nathan asked. 'What's happened?'

Mum made a smug face. 'Got a job, haven't I? Down the supermarket, with Nads. I start Monday.'

Nathan, vastly relieved that it was nothing to do with Brian, got himself a Coke and prised open the ring-pull. 'Cheers, then. That's great.' Perhaps Natalie had made it up after all, about seeing Mum in the pub. It was exactly the sort of thing she *would* invent.

'Aren't Nadia and Owen coming over?' he asked.

'No, not till Sunday. Nads is working tonight and tomorrow,' Mum said.

'I'm staying the weekend with Dad. You haven't forgotten, have you?'

Mum laughed. 'Forgotten? With you reminding me at least five times a day? Some chance.'

Later, when they'd eaten, Nathan went upstairs to get his things ready. Nine o'clock, Dad had said, but he wanted to make sure everything was ready in good time. He put out his best sweatshirt and jeans, to wear to Alton Towers tomorrow; in a Sainsbury's carrier bag he put a T-shirt, clean underwear, toothbrush and deodorant, and a couple of cassettes.

Homework. He had Geography and Science to do over the weekend. Better do it tonight, because Nadia was sure to ask when he came back on Sunday, and he didn't know how late he'd be. He took his books and pencil-case downstairs. Mum was watching TV, some Friday night rubbish, but she'd tidied away the tea things and brought in a tray with coffee and biscuits on it.

'Blimey!' she said, seeing the school books. 'You feeling all right? Never known you do homework on a Friday night before.'

'Want to get it out of the way,' Nathan said. He could have asked *her* if she was feeling all right, too. Normally by now she was slumped on the settee with her packet of fags and her cans of lager, and the air full of smoke.

'You given up smoking?' he asked her.

'Cutting down. Nads don't like it, not with Katy. You know, all this fuss about passive smoking and all that. Bad for kids especially.'

Nathan thought of all the smoke he must have inhaled, over the years of living with Mum and Smudge, and nobody caring. Still, it made sense. It was obvious that babies shouldn't breathe in smoke.

'Got much?' Mum said.

'No.' Nathan spread out his books on the coffee-table and started work, with half his attention on the television. Really, it was making him feel bad, all this attention and concern from Mum. What would she say when he told her he was moving out to live with Dad? He'd always thought she'd be glad to see the back of him; but now she was definitely making an effort. Perhaps she'd been to the doctor after all, got herself some pills or something to cheer herself up. All this couldn't be down to getting a job in the supermarket. It was only checkout work, after all.

*

In the morning he woke early, eager to get on with his day. Smudge was snoring quietly from the other bed, and sunshine was pushing its way through the curtains – it was going to be hot. Moving about quietly so as not to wake Smudge, he showered and dressed, then went down to make tea and toast. He'd never been so organised. His homework was all done, his school bag packed ready for Monday. It was easy, really.

Mum came down, yawning in her dressing-gown, while he was eating his toast.

'Make me a coffee, will you?' she asked, lighting a cigarette.

Nathan looked at her suspiciously, remembering last night, and the good mood she'd been in. He wouldn't have been surprised to find her back to normal today: spending all day in her dressing-gown, watching TV through a haze of smoke. 'Thought you were cutting down,' he said.

'Got to have something to get me started.' Mum inhaled deeply, wandered over to the window and looked out. 'Looks like a nice day. Barry taking you anywhere special?'

'Mum!' he reproached her. 'I told you – we're going to Alton Towers!'

'Oh, right. Remember last time?' She smiled at him. 'Going on that – what's it called – Log Flume? And Smudge going green?'

He refilled the kettle and made the coffee, adding two spoonfuls of sugar. He wondered whether Dad would come into the house, like last time. At least, if he did, he wouldn't argue with Mum today – she didn't look in the mood for arguing. She was up earlier than usual, and had already brushed her hair. Perhaps, though, it would be better if Dad didn't see her looking so much better. Better if Dad carried on thinking she was always in a state, like last week…

The phone rang.

'I'll get it,' Mum said quickly.

She went into the front room. Nathan followed, with the coffee mug. Mum sat down on the settee, curling up her legs in expectation of a long chat.

'Hello?' she said, in a soft voice. Then it changed. 'Oh. Barry.'

Dad. Probably phoning to say he was leaving, or to check that Nathan was up.

'No, I was expecting someone else, that's all,' Mum said. Then, after a pause: 'Oh. Oh. I see. Yes, he's here. Do you want to talk to him yourself? OK then. Yeah, I'll tell him. Yeah, bye.' She put the phone down, and sipped at the coffee Nathan handed her, not looking at him.

'What did he want?' Nathan asked.

'Sorry, Nathe,' Mum said. 'He can't make it after all.'

'*What?*' Nathan couldn't take in what she was saying. 'What d'you mean? What did he say? Is he coming later?'

'Not coming at all. Sorry, love. I know you must be disappointed.'

Mum hadn't called him 'love' for ages. He stared at her.

'Why? Why not? What did he *say*?'

Mum blew out cigarette smoke. 'Something else came up, that's all he said. Sorry, love. That's tough.'

If she said sorry once more, if she kept on smoking and calling him love and saying sorry, he was going to hit her.

'Something else? What sort of something else?' he demanded.

'How should I know? Work, I suppose.'

Nathan just stood there, all the excitement draining out of him, leaving something that felt like a sick black hollow space inside. He had a choky feeling in his throat. Dad hadn't even bothered to *speak* to him, even though Mum had said he was here! Couldn't be bothered to spend one minute explaining, saying he was sorry – he hadn't even said they'd go tomorrow instead, or next weekend—

Something else came up.

Work? Or fun?

Suddenly Nathan thought of that blonde woman,

from the flat above. Kim, with her spiky high heels and her blonde frizz of hair and her sparkly jumper that made her look like a Christmas decoration. Nathan felt certain that Kim was the *something else* that had come up. Something more interesting. Something more worthwhile. Dad had more time for Kim than for Nathan – he'd proved that, last week. Nathan felt a blaze of jealous hatred. He found he was clenching his teeth tightly. If he unclenched them, he'd shout, or cry.

'I expect he'll take you out another day,' Mum said, dropping ash on the carpet and not noticing. 'Just like bloody Barry, to say he'll do something and then not. Christ knows I had enough of that when I was with him. So no Alton Towers after all. What a shame.'

She didn't understand. She didn't understand at all. She thought it was only missing Alton Towers that mattered. Why were grown-ups so *stupid?*

He just stood there. It seemed pointless to sit down, pointless to go up to his room. The weekend he had been looking forward to was a blank space, a featureless stretch of time to be filled somehow.

Mum looked at him. 'Why don't you go up to that animal place of yours?'

'Why?' Nathan said, suspicious.

'Well, the thing is, I've got Brian coming round later on.' Mum gave an embarrassed laugh. 'I mean, you could stay here, but you'd probably rather be out of it.'

Brian!

Natalie hadn't been lying after all. Brian would be coming round here with his fat stomach and his loud laugh and his sweaty face. Brian would be loafing on the settee and smoking and watching videos. Brian would go up to Mum's bedroom with her.

'But I thought – Nadia told me – Brian's married,' Nathan blurted, 'and his wife found out about – about him and you. About him coming here. That was why he stopped coming.'

'Yeah, well, that was then. He's left his wife now,' Mum said. There was a smile on the edge of her mouth, a pleased, smug smile.

The hollow inside Nathan grew bigger and darker, big enough to swallow him up. All the effort Mum had made yesterday had been for Brian, not for him at all. The hoovering, the cleaning, the strawberry cheesecake, the brushed hair and the smiles – all for Brian. Mum was too busy with Brian, Dad was too busy with Kim – neither of them had time for him. He was in the way. Brian had left his wife, for Mum. He'd be moving in next.

'I'm going up to Windfall,' he said. He could hardly get the words out. Something was pressing on his chest, choking him.

'OK, love,' Mum said. 'See you later, then. What time'll you be back – six, seven?'

'Never!' Nathan tried to shout, but his voice came out all throttled and choked. The way he felt.

He banged his way outside and lunged for Saskia's bike, grazing the knuckles of one hand on the wall. Sucking at the skinned place, he unlocked the bike and dragged it round to the front. Then, without knowing where he was going, he mounted it and rode off, pedalling as hard as he could.

Breakfast Upstairs

He was panting, leaning forward over the handlebars to coax maximum speed out of Saskia's bike, but he didn't know where to go.

Windfall? He could go there, but he'd told Saskia and Simon, and even Tessa, about his weekend with Dad – if he went there now, he'd have to explain that it had all fallen through, that Dad didn't care about him.

He had to see Dad. He had to know what Dad was doing. He took the road out of town and headed towards Beckley. His legs ached and his throat was sore and something inside was trying to strangle him, but he cycled all the way there without stopping. By the time he reached Dad's flat, and flung the bike down outside the dry cleaner's, he was wondering why he'd been so stupid as to come here. Perhaps Dad had had to work today, do driving lessons. *Something came up*. That could easily mean work, couldn't it? One of the other instructors was ill, and

Dad had to work instead. That would make sense. They'd go to Alton Towers next weekend, and everything would be all right.

Having convinced himself that Dad wouldn't be in, he went upstairs anyway and rang the doorbell to Dad's flat. Nothing. He rang twice more, and waited. Then he heard movement in the flat above.

That woman, Kim. She was in. Maybe she'd know where Dad was. He could go up and ask her, and she'd say, 'Barry had to work,' and then he'd know. He could phone Dad later and arrange about next weekend, and then he could go to Windfall for the day. There'd still be Brian at home, but at least he'd have next weekend to look forward to.

He ran up the flight of stairs. Kim's front door had a fancy knocker and a spyhole. The doorbell played a jingly tune, and when it stopped Nathan heard voices inside the flat. Then a shadow came towards the spy hole and he heard Kim saying, 'Looks like Nathan! Thought you said he wasn't coming?'

Nathan stood there, staring at the spyhole, willing himself through it and into Kim's flat. Another part of him wanted to run downstairs, out into the street. He wanted to kick out, throw things, break something. Then the door opened and Kim stood there with her blonde frizz of hair, her mouth stretching in a fake smile.

'Hi! You'd better come in,' she said.

They were having breakfast, Kim and Dad, in the lounge with the TV on. They'd been sitting together on the sofa; there were plates of toast and mugs of coffee on the floor. Dad hadn't shaved yet. He stood up when Nathan came in and brushed toast crumbs off his jeans.

'Hi, Nathan,' he said. 'Sorry about today.'

Nathan just stared. His fists tightened; he felt like punching Dad. And Kim. He wanted to hurt them, both of them.

'Er – it's Kim's birthday today, you see,' Dad said. 'I only found out yesterday.'

He was lying. Nathan could tell, from the edginess in his voice, the way his eyes slid to Kim's face, as if he was telling her, *It's your birthday, OK?* Nathan looked at the mantelpiece. No cards.

'Dad,' Nathan said. Instead of being angry, his voice came out as a childish plea. 'I've got to talk to you. Got to tell you something.'

Dad made a hopeless gesture with his hands, looking at Kim. She said, 'I'll make you some toast, Nathan, OK? And a cup of tea.'

He shook his head. He didn't want toast, he'd choke if he tried to eat; but Kim went out anyway and closed the door. Dad sat on the sofa and gestured to Nathan to sit down too. Kim's flat was the same as Dad's, but much more cluttered, with squashy chairs and lots of velvet cushions.

'Look, I'm sorry about today,' Dad said again. 'I didn't mean to let you down. We'll go next weekend, OK?'

'You didn't even speak to me,' Nathan said, in a tight voice. 'On the phone. I was there, but you just gave Mum a message.'

'I felt bad about it, OK?' Dad said. 'Only – well, Kim's a good friend, and she was going to spend her birthday on her own. I didn't think you'd mind that much if I put our weekend off.'

'If you'd *said*—' Nathan began. But he would have minded anyway. Kim was more important than he was – that was what Dad was saying. This was supposed to have been a special weekend.

But there was no point getting angry with Dad.

He started again. 'Dad. I specially wanted to see you today, because – well, because—'

'Yeah?' Dad picked up his half-eaten toast and started crunching it.

Nathan took a deep breath. 'It's awful at home. Really awful. I can't stay there. You know that fat bloke Brian? He's started coming round again. Coming round today. He's left his wife, Mum says. So he'll be round our place all the time, now. I hate him, Dad, I really hate him!'

He wanted Dad to look at him, but Dad bent down and picked up his mug of coffee.

'Dad,' Nathan pleaded. 'Can't I come and live with you? You've got a spare room. I can cycle to school from here. I won't be any trouble, honest! I could do things for you when you're at work, get the shopping, get our tea—'

Dad did look at him now. He stared, his eyes widening in surprise. Then he shook his head in disbelief. He gave a short huff of a laugh, and looked at Nathan as if he expected him to laugh too.

'Whoa! Hang on there a minute. Move in? Move in here?' He shook his head again like a dog shaking water from its ears. 'Sorry, Nathe. No way. I can't be doing with – I mean, I'm too busy, I work long hours, I never know whether I'm coming or going. You wouldn't like it. You'd be stuck here on your own most of the time. You—'

'Please, Dad. I wouldn't mind being on my own. I'd have—' He'd have Hazel, but he'd better not mention that just yet. 'I've got friends in Beckley. It wouldn't matter. Go on, say yes, *please*!'

Dad took a deep gulp of coffee, swallowed, then shook his head again, firmly. 'No. Sorry, Nathe, but there it is. Things'll get better at home. At least Nina – at least Mum'll pull herself together a bit, if she's got Brian back.'

'But I hate Brian! I can't stay there with him around!'

'He can't be that bad. No one's that bad. You'll get used to him.'

'I don't want to get used to him! I want to get used to *you*!' Nathan heard himself sounding more and more childish. He'd start crying in a minute. And that wouldn't do anything to soften Dad, he knew that.

'No, Nathan,' Dad said in a stern voice. 'Sorry, but no.'

Nathan stood up. His eyes were blurring over, and Dad's face swam in front of him. 'You don't care about me!' he blurted out. 'You can't be bothered! You've got time for tarty old Kim but not for me. You don't give a toss—'

'Hang on a minute. Don't get yourself worked up. Sit down, we can talk things over—'

'Forget it! What's the point?'

Nathan turned for the door, colliding with Kim, who was coming in with a plate of toast and a mug of coffee. He barged past, knocking her out of his way. Coffee sloshed over the door and the toast slapped down on the carpet.

'Hey, watch it!' Kim gasped. 'What's biting you?'

'Piss off!' Nathan yelled back. He fumbled with the front door catch, let himself out and ran downstairs. In the entrance at the bottom he waited for a second

– a stupid, idiotic part of him was expecting Dad to run down after him, calling, 'Nathan, come back. Don't go. I've changed my mind.'

Dad did no such thing. No one followed. Dad was no doubt too busy comforting Kim, helping to clear up the mess, apologising for Nathan's yobbishness.

Nathan went out into the street and slammed the door behind him. 'I hate you!' he yelled. Then he picked up a Coke can that was lying by the wall and hurled it as hard as he could against the bus shelter. An old lady walking by on the opposite side of the road stopped to look at him, tutting. For a second he thought of shouting something rude, but then his anger fizzled out and he felt more like crying. Really crying, blubbing like a little kid.

He got back on his bike and cycled down the High Street, slowly and drearily. He couldn't go back to Dad's and he couldn't go home. Where now?

There was only Windfall. Windfall, and Saskia and Hazel. Hazel would be pleased to see him. People might not be trustworthy or loyal, but dogs were.

Rehomed

He cycled furiously up the hill, veered through the gateway and skidded to a halt, seeing Simon and Saskia just inside. They were kneeling by a freshly-dug strip of earth, planting out lettuces. One glance at the companionable way they were kneeling together with the tray of lettuces between them was enough to tell him they'd made up their quarrel. He got off and wiped his face. He was hot and sweaty, and his legs were wobbly from all the cycling he'd done, at a faster speed than he'd known he could manage.

'Hello!' Saskia called, standing up. 'Didn't think you were coming today!'

'No. Well.' He stared at them, a new disappointment growing. He'd have preferred their argument to last, to split them up; he didn't want Saskia to spend her time with Simon. 'It didn't work out,' he managed. The lump in his throat choked off any other words he might have tried to say.

Then Simon stood up too, looked at Saskia and said, 'Why don't we all go and look at the donkey?'

'Why?' Nathan said suspiciously. They hadn't nearly finished with the lettuces; there were two more trays still to be planted out.

'Good idea,' Saskia said.

Nathan parked his bike by the office. Usually, he went straight in to see Hazel; he glanced towards her shed and saw Tessa standing just inside the doorway, with two other people, a man and a woman. They must have come to look at one of the dogs in there. He'd better stay out of the way.

The sun was beating down hard on the paddock, but Orsino, not seeming to mind, was grazing near the gateway, not down in the shady place at the bottom. He came up as they approached, and Simon reached out a hand to scratch him behind the ears.

'He's all right, isn't he?' Nathan said.

'Yes. But there's been a bit of trouble,' Saskia told him. 'Tessa found out. The owners came down here last night to see if she knew where he was, and she was just in the middle of saying she hadn't even seen a donkey, when – would you believe it – he started braying! Hee-hawing at the top of his voice.' She giggled uneasily. 'There was a hell of a row. They accused her of stealing him and then – well – Simon had to tell her it was me who'd taken him. And you.'

'Oh. So now what?' Nathan asked, thinking fast. 'Is that why you've brought me down here? To get me out of Tessa's way? Has she said I'm not allowed up here any more, or what?'

'No. There's something else we've got to tell you,' Simon said.

'What?' Nathan's thoughts raced. Mrs Briand? Police?

'It's about Hazel,' Simon said. 'There are some people here who want a dog like Hazel. They came yesterday to look at her and now they've made their mind up. Tessa went round earlier to do a home check and they're collecting her now.'

The words jumbled themselves in Nathan's head. He tried to clutch at their sense. 'Have her, collect her? Take Hazel away?' he burst out. 'How can they? She's mine!'

Saskia wasn't even looking at him.

'I know how you feel,' Simon said. 'We all get fond of the animals here – too fond, sometimes – and you've worked hard with Hazel. But she's *not* yours, Nathan, and you've got to realise, it's much better for her to be rehomed. Tessa says these people are just right for her.'

Nathan stared back. 'But she's *my* dog! No one else can have her!'

He had to stop this from happening – no one could

give Hazel away! He turned and ran back to the yard, into the dog house, where Tessa was standing by the open door to Hazel's pen. Hazel was on a lead, sittting just inside the door, her ears pressed back. She looked uneasy, but she was sitting obediently, the way he'd taught her. Seeing him, she wriggled and gave a *wuff* of recognition. That proved it. She was his dog. He went straight to her; she pressed herself against his legs.

'Oh, Nathan,' Tessa said, looking embarrassed. 'I didn't think you were coming today. This is the boy I was telling you about,' she said to the visitors, 'who's done so much work with Hazel—'

'You were going to give her away,' Nathan burst out, 'without even telling me! I'd have come back and found her gone— You can't give her away! She's *my* dog!'

'Oh dear. This must be very upsetting for you,' said the woman. Nathan glared at her. She had a face that looked quite young till you noticed the lines round her eyes and mouth. The man with her looked sympathetic too; they were nice, kind people. Just the sort of people to give a dog a good home.

'Nathan, listen,' Tessa said. 'It's much better for Hazel to go and live with Mr and Mrs Hoyle than to stay here penned up most of the day. You know that. They understand that she needs careful handling.

They know she's been mistreated. They're prepared to take trouble with her. They've had dogs before. It's the ideal home for her, Nathan.'

No, it wasn't! *He* was the right person for Hazel. Without him, she wouldn't be sitting there wearing a collar and lead, waiting to be led away. Without him she'd still be biting and snarling and cringing. He opened his mouth to protest, and a desperate sound came out. He'd made her better, improved her, and his only reward was to see her taken away by complete strangers! It wasn't *fair* – he felt like snarling, biting someone. He loved her, and she loved him—

'You'd be welcome to come and see her,' the man was saying, but Nathan could only stare at Hazel's face, her trusting eyes, her tawny eyebrows that twitched as she gazed back at him. His eyes filled with tears. For a second, he thought of snatching the lead from Tessa's hand and running away with Hazel.

But where to?

He made a strangled sound in his throat, gave Hazel a last anguished look and ran out into the sunshine. He had to get away.

'Nathan, wait!' Tessa called out. Ignoring her, he ran to the office. Saskia was sitting on the step, waiting for him, but without looking at her he yanked the bike upright, threw his leg over and pedalled out of the yard. Riding away fast, he felt his eyes blurring, and the tears leaked and blew back into his ears. He wanted to howl his misery into the summer sky, shout out the injustice of it all.

They were taking his dog. His Hazel.

Dad didn't want him, and now he had no Hazel. And no Windfall, since he didn't think he could ever bear to go there again, with Hazel's cage empty. They'd deceived him, all of them. They'd have given Hazel away without even giving him the chance to say goodbye. He hated them.

He was speeding downhill like an arrow, not knowing where to go or why. He should have turned in the opposite direction, headed out along the country lanes, where no one could find him. Where no one would see if he cried.

But the bike was carrying him back towards the town. The town centre on Saturday would be crowded: little kids running round, families, teenagers hanging around the precinct. There would be people he knew, and he didn't want to see anyone he knew. Only Smudge. Smudge would be on his stall at the Saturday market.

Nathan rode into town as far as he could get, into the pedestrianised precinct where he had to swerve round people pushing baby buggies. Someone tutted at him, yanking a toddler out of his path. Then, seeing a policeman, Nathan dismounted and pushed the bike the rest of the way to the market square.

In the hot sunshine, the market had the atmosphere of a summer fair. People were walking about in shorts and sleeveless tops, and some were sitting on the steps by the fountain, with their legs stretched out. There was an ice-cream cart and a stand with striped awnings that sold cold drinks. The sun made everyone slow down, saunter round the stalls, linger in the shade. All the stallholders were cheerful on a day like this, because it meant good sales. Nathan parked the bike in a narrow alleyway and went to find Smudge.

Trev – sleeveless leather jerkin, hair slicked back, spotty chin – was there today. Smudge was counting out change, but he saw Nathan out of the corner of his eye.

'Watcha, bruv! Thought you were with Barry today?' he called, as soon as his customer went away. Theirs was one of the noisiest stalls, with music pounding from a pair of speakers. Trev was singing along and eyeing a group of girls who seemed about to come over.

'S'posed to be, wasn't I? He couldn't make it.'

Nathan didn't feel like telling Smudge the whole story – about Dad's lies, about Kim. Not with Trev standing there.

'Oh, tough,' Smudge said. 'What, was he working?'

Nathan shrugged. 'Something like that.' Then, not really meaning to, he found himself adding, 'He hasn't got time for us. Not any more,' in a kind of appeal to Smudge. He wanted Smudge to share his disappointment.

'No, well,' Smudge said. 'It ent as if he's our real dad. Now he's not with Mum, he needn't have nothing to do with us if he don't want to. Want to get us a burger? Get one for yourself an' all.' He fished into his money belt and gave Nathan a five-pound note.

Nathan took the note and wandered over to the burger van, dodging between rows of stalls as he saw Eduardo with some other boys from school. 'Not as if he's our real dad'. No. Nathan had almost forgotten. He'd almost made himself believe that Barry *was* his dad.

'I've got the boy here for the day'. That was what Dad – Barry – had said to Kim, that first time. Not 'I've got my boy here', or 'my son'. Nathan thought of Barry as Dad, but to Barry he was just *the boy*. Nina's boy. Troublesome, a bit of a pain. Always wanting something.

Nathan thought about his real father. He'd left home so long ago that Nathan couldn't remember him, didn't know what he looked like. Neil, his name was: Nathan knew that. They were all 'N's in their family. Nathan's real father had left when Nathan was three, for Liverpool. He still lived there. Mum got monthly payments from him but had never seen him since, and Barry had moved in soon after. All three children – Nadia, Smudge and Nathan – had grown up calling Barry their dad, though they all knew he wasn't. Nathan was the only one who still called him Dad.

Nathan paid for Smudge's hamburger but couldn't face one himself. He'd throw up if he tried to swallow, and anyway he was supposed to be off meat. There must be something wrong with him. His real dad hadn't wanted him, and now neither did Barry. There was something about him that drove dads away. Smudge didn't mind much, and neither did Nadia, but then they both had lives of their own: Nadia had Owen and Katy; Smudge had Cheryl. Smudge could probably move out and shack up with Cheryl if he got really fed up with things at home. But Smudge didn't mind Brian the way Nathan did.

He was never going to call anyone else Dad, that was definite. He'd had two goes at dads and he wasn't having a third. Not if the only choice was a slob like Brian.

He'd sooner leave home and sleep in a cardboard box.

Clown

The hamburger napkin was warmly soggy in Nathan's hand as he walked slowly back to Smudge's stall. The smell of meat and onions was making him feel hungry, but he'd be sick if he tried to eat. The black hollow was there inside, gnawing. Eating him.

What now? He supposed he could go back to the stall and help out, stay there all day if he liked, but then what?

The idea of running away from home had taken root in his mind. What did he have to lose? He could hitch-hike to London, find out where people his age hung around. These May nights were warm enough to sleep out. He could go just as he was, not bothering to go home for extra clothes or a toothbrush. Mum probably wouldn't bother to report him missing, and once he was there he could pass for sixteen. Maybe earn some money somehow, find a hostel or a squat to live in. He'd never have to go to school again…

Damien had been reading a book about a boy who lived rough in London. *Stone Cold,* it was called; Nathan remembered the cover picture. There was a murderer – a pervert, an older bloke who picked up young boys and offered them shelter, then stabbed them and hid their bodies under the floorboards.

Asleep in a shop doorway you'd be vulnerable. Anyone could come along and mug you or knife you or steal what little you had. The idea of running away sounded exciting at first, but not when you thought about the details. What would you eat? Where would you go to the bog? And how would you survive in winter when the temperature dropped below zero? He pictured himself frozen to death in a cardboard box. That'd show Mum, if she ever found out. And Barry. And Tessa. Serve them right.

A crowd of people had gathered round the fountain. There were often buskers here on a Saturday, but Nathan couldn't see what was going on for the press of people. Then a clown's head in a pointed hat with a bobble on top rose above the circle of watchers' heads, and some taped music started up. Owen!

Nathan ran back to deliver the hamburger. 'Owen's over there, doing his clown act,' he told Smudge.

'Want to come and see?'

'No, I've seen him enough times,' Smudge said, rearranging CDs in a box. 'You go if you want.'

Nathan had seen Owen many times too, but he felt himself pulled into the circle of watchers. Owen wore his pink and orange clown costume and his enormous black shoes with curled-up toes; he'd painted his face in a wistful expression, and the pointed hat, ridiculously tiny, was balanced on his springy hair. He was doing one of the routines Nathan had seen before, one in which he tried to train an invisible but awkward dog. Nathan wished Owen had chosen one of his other routines, but he couldn't help staying to watch, mesmerised. Owen had the ability to create a scene all on his own, using taped music, his actions and his imagination. He saw the invisible dog himself, and the power of his vision was enough to make everyone in the audience see it too, and know what it was doing. Silently, Owen told the dog to sit, smiled as it did so and patted its head, then started to walk away, turning every few steps. The dog sat still for a few moments, then ran up to Owen, weaving through his legs and making him teeter wildly for balance. Next, Owen tried to make it walk at heel, shuffling along in his enormous shoes. The dog dodged from one side of him to the other, then sat down and refused to move. Owen then produced an imaginary lead and clipped that to the dog's collar. After a few satisfactory steps, the dog zoomed round Owen, entangling him in the lead until he was tied up like a parcel.

Nathan joined in the applause at the end, surprised to find himself smiling broadly. Watching Owen was like coming back from free-spinning in the darkness of outer space, back to the gravitational pull of normality. Someone threw a scatter of coins into the empty violin-case Owen carried with him. Owen bowed, pretended to be overcome with bashfulness, and then caught Nathan's eye. Nathan expected him to change his tape and go into another routine, but instead he came over.

Owen's voice came from the painted clown mouth. 'I thought you were spending the weekend with Barry? Is he here?'

'No. He couldn't make it. He phoned this morning.'

'Oh, Christ.' Owen sounded deeply disappointed. 'What are you doing, then?'

'Just hanging around.'

Nathan couldn't keep control of his own mouth, which was twisting itself into strange shapes. His eyes blurred over and Owen's clown face swam in front of him. It was an odd sensation anyway, talking to Owen with his make-up on; you had to stare to find

Owen's real eyes beneath the clown's big sad ones, and his mouth inside the wide banana-shape painted in orangey-red and outlined in black.

'Come on,' Owen said briskly. He bent down to snap the violin case shut, and picked up his cassette player.

'What, have you finished?'

'I have now. Come on. We're going to get something to eat.'

'But I—'

'Come on,' Owen said, jerking his head with the silly pointed hat on.

They walked through the precinct together. People turned to look at them and laugh. It was one thing for Owen to charm his audience; something else for a clown to be walking unselfconsciously past the rows of shops, chatting. Owen led the way into Pizza Hut and found the only empty table. People looked at him in expectation of a stand-up comedy act or a charity collection. Owen sat down, taking up a lot of space in his squashy trousers.

'You ought to be busking. You're losing money, sitting in here,' Nathan said.

'Yeah, well.' The clown smile stretched. 'Earn it to spend it, don't I? This is on me.' He held up the menu in white-gloved hands, and ordered, very solemnly, from a giggling waitress. When the table was loaded with drinks, pizzas and salad, he said, 'Now come on, tell me about it.'

Nathan shrugged. 'There's nothing else to tell.'

But he found himself telling Owen everything – about Dad, and Kim, and Hazel being rehomed, and about Mum and Brian. Even about his real dad. Even about his idea of running away to London. Owen listened, and ate, and nodded, and looked at Nathan with his sad clown eyes, with their eyebrows that kinked right up into his hair.

'Mummy! That clown's eating pizza!' a little girl shouted from a nearby table.

'Clowns need to eat, same as everyone else,' a parental voice replied.

Afterwards, they went back to the flat where Owen lived with Nadia and Katy. Nadia was working till six o'clock, and Katy was with her child-minder. Nathan waited while Owen changed and took off his make-up. The flat was much smaller than Dad's, and the back windows looked out at tatty brick sheds behind the shops, but it was neat and cheerful, with postcards Blu-tacked to the walls, a checked cloth on the table and coloured patchwork cushions on the tiny sofa. Owen came out of the bathroom looking very scrubbed and bare and normal, though with traces of greasepaint clinging to his hair.

'I'm going to collect Katy, then we'll take her to

the park, shall we?' he said.

Katy's child-minder lived a few streets away, in a row of houses that backed on to the canal. A smiling middle-aged woman opened the door, and Owen surprised Nathan by kissing her on the cheek and saying, 'Hi, Mum.'

Inside, Katy was sitting on the carpet, clutching a piece of plastic puzzle. 'Owid! Owid!' she cried delightedly, holding out her arms to him. He picked her up and swung her high while she giggled, then he lowered her and kissed the top of her hair.

'Mum, this is Nathan,' Owen said. 'We're going to take Katy to the park.'

'I'll come too,' Owen's mum said. 'It's a lovely afternoon.'

Half an hour later they were down by the lake, helping Katy to throw bread to the ducks. Nathan wished Owen's mum hadn't come; to be honest, he wished Katy wasn't there, either. He wanted Owen to himself. There wasn't any more to say, but just being with Owen made him feel better. He watched Owen pull Katy into his arms as a quacking duck came too close, frightening her, and knew it was hopeless. This was just for now. Anyone looking at them would think what a happy family they were – a mum out with her two sons and much younger daughter, perhaps, or a very young dad with his two children and their gran. It wasn't *fair*. Katy had no proper dad, either. But she had Owen, who loved her more than either of Nathan's dads loved him.

Nathan picked up a stone and hurled it into the water.

At the end of today, when Owen took Katy home, he would still be alone.

But while he was with them and Katy and the sun was shining, he could pretend. On the way home, Katy fell asleep in her buggy, and they all went back to Owen's mum's house and sat in the garden by the canal, and had choc-ices from the freezer. After a while Owen fell asleep too, with his face to the sun and his mouth open. His mum started doing a bit of weeding, and Nathan wandered down to the canal and looked for fish, and watched narrow boats going by. Later, Owen's mum made a pot of tea and brought out cake on a tray; Owen jerked awake, looking dopey and embarrassed, and Katy woke up too and wanted Nathan to help her look for butterflies. It was all so *easy*. No one shouted or got in a strop or sulked. This was what being in a family must be like.

When they'd had their tea, Owen looked at his watch and said to Nathan, 'It's time we were getting back. Nadia comes home just after six.'

'OK,' Nathan said.

That was it. The pretending was over. He didn't

belong here, didn't belong anywhere. Owen had been great, but he hadn't actually come up with any answers. How could he? There weren't any answers. Owen had enough responsibilities of his own, considering he was only twenty-one.

'Bye, love. Come again,' his mum said to Nathan.

He walked along beside Owen and the buggy in silence.

Then Owen looked at him and said, 'We've got a spare room. You can stay the night if you want.'

Family

'Here you are, sleepyhead.' Nadia plonked a mug of tea on the floor next to the mattress Nathan was sleeping on. 'I'm surprised Katy didn't wake you up – she's been singing at the top of her voice since about seven. I'll get you some breakfast when you're up.'

Nathan rolled over and looked at the strange room, lying on his back with his hands linked behind his head. There was just about room for a mattress on the floor, squeezed in beside the window and a pile of boxes with a lamp teetering on top. Nadia and Owen hadn't lived here long, and their own bedroom – only big enough for their bed and Katy's crib – didn't run to a wardrobe, so all their clothes were piled in a massive heap on a chair in here, with a jumble of shoes underneath. If Nathan wanted to close the door, he'd have to shove the chair out of the way first, so he hadn't bothered.

They were all going round to Mum's later on.

They'd agreed that last night. Nathan wasn't looking forward to it at all. He sat up to drink his tea, and listened to Owen singing 'Yellow Submarine' for Katy, and Nadia laughing and joining in the chorus.

He had slept heavily, late. By the time Owen had gone out for milk and the Sunday papers, and they'd eaten breakfast – all sitting together round the table – and Nadia had sorted out Katy and strapped her into the buggy, it was nearly eleven. All the same, the curtains were drawn at home. It took some while for Mum to appear at the front door, clutching her dressing-gown so that it didn't sag open.

'God, you're early,' she yawned. 'Come on in and I'll get some coffee going.'

They all went inside, and Mum pulled the curtains open. There were empty glasses on the coffee-table and all the ashtrays were full. The room stank of smoke. Nadia coughed pointedly. 'Katy can't stay in here, breathing this. It smells like a pub the morning after. Why don't you take her out the back, Owen? I'll do the coffee, Mum, if you go and get dressed.'

Last night it had all seemed so easy. Now, back home, Nathan felt depression seep into him along with the stale smoke. This was where he lived. He'd never get away. Mum was still his mum, and she'd never let him. He went into the kitchen with Nadia and rummaged around to find enough clean mugs, washing up the dirty ones in the sink. Nadia, Owen, Mum, himself. And one more. Five mugs of coffee. Heavy footsteps creaked on the ceiling over his head, and he heard a deep male voice.

They took the tray into the tatty square of garden. Nathan thought of Owen's mum's, yesterday afternoon – not a fussy garden, but one where things grew, a garden someone cared for. This was just a patchy lawn, bordered by a fence that sagged. A cracked concrete path led down one side and there was a dustbin outside the back door with its lid missing, so that paper and shreds of wrapping material strayed on to the lawn. It was the sort of patch that looked ripe for one of those TV gardening teams to burst in, laying proper paths and putting up trellises and plonking down urns that overflowed with flowers and ivy. Except that Mum wouldn't see the point of such a transformation. She hardly stepped outside, unless to put something in the dustbin.

'What's the point of sitting out here?' Mum said, seeing the others sitting on the grass. She had taken some while to get dressed, putting on black velvet trousers, sandals with high heels, a tight pink T-shirt and quite a lot of make-up. She went back indoors, brought out a cushion and placed it on the grass, sitting down with exaggerated care.

Nadia passed her a mug. 'We're not staying today, Mum. Just came round to sort things out.'

'What things?' Mum had brought out cigarettes and a lighter, and now she opened the packet and lit up. 'Anyway, it's just as well you're not staying. Brian and me are going out to meet some friends of his.'

'Mum, we think Nathan ought to come and stay with us,' Nadia said firmly. 'We've come to collect some of his things.'

Mum inhaled deeply, then looked sideways at Nadia. 'Stay? How d'you mean, stay? How long?'

'Live with us,' Owen said. 'We want him to come and live with us.'

Mum pulled a sceptical face. 'What, in that poky flat? You joking? Hardly got room for yourselves, I'd have thought.'

'We can manage,' Nadia said.

'And you really want to be bothered?' Mum said, blowing smoke and tilting her head to watch it rise into the still air. 'I'd have thought you had enough on your plates as it is.'

'Yes. We can be bothered,' Owen said. It was the first time Nathan had ever heard him speak sharply. 'Not that Nathan *is* any bother, are you, Nathe?'

Mum looked at him in surprise. Owen, sprawling, continued laying out pieces of a plastic puzzle for Katy. Nathan didn't say anything, but sat tearing blades of grass out of the sparse lawn.

'You just wait, if you think he's no bother,' Mum said, with a humourless laugh. 'You wait till you get the school on the phone every day, saying he's run off or been rude or got in a fight. What are you anyway?' she asked Owen. 'A one-man adoption agency?'

'Nathan will be happier with us, that's all,' Nadia said. 'He doesn't want to stay here, not with—'

Then she stopped, as Brian stepped out into the garden and looked at the assembled group on the grass. Nathan looked at him in distaste. He was a big, flabby man, with trousers that sagged below the swell of his stomach, and a purple polo shirt that stretched over it. He hadn't shaved, and to Nathan he always looked sweaty and dirty. How *could* Mum…? What did she see in him? Why did she think it was worth dressing up and putting on make-up, to impress this slob of a man?

'What's this, a garden party?' Brian said, and then in a posh voice, 'Oh dear, I would have made cucumber sandwiches. Where's the butler?'

'Come and sit down, love,' Mum said, in a completely changed voice. 'Nadia's made you coffee.'

Brian looked surprised, but he came over and lowered himself to sit on the ground.

'What's this then?' he asked again. 'Family conference?'

'Yes,' Nadia said. 'We were just talking about—'

'They want to take my Nathe away from me,' Mum said. She leaned close to Brian and clasped his arm.

'Yeah?' Brian thought it was a good idea, Nathan could tell. 'Take him where?'

'Are you moving in, then?' Owen asked Brian.

'Well, yeah,' Brian said, putting an arm round Mum. 'That's what Nina wants, isn't it, Neen? I've split up with the wife now, and me and Neen want to make a go of it. All right with you, is it?' he added, with an aggressive jut of his chin.

'I'm glad things are working out for you, Mum,' Nadia said tactfully. 'With the job, and now Brian moving in. You certainly seem a lot happier. That's great. But we've got to sort something out for Nathan, something that's going to work. He can't go on as things are.'

Brian settled himself more comfortably. 'From what you say, Neen, the boy's nothing but a blasted nuisance anyway. Always getting himself into trouble. If Nadia and her bloke here want to have a go, well let them.'

'There's nothing wrong with Nathan,' Owen said.

Nathan remembered the play-fights, the way Brian would twist his arm behind his back and give it that extra tug, to show that he could hurt him if he wanted to. Before, Nathan had never been left alone in the house with Brian. He wouldn't want to be. Brian's surface good-humour wasn't trustworthy. Would he ever hurt Mum? Nathan didn't like thinking about that; but at least she had the choice. It was her house – she could throw Brian out if she wanted to.

Mum turned to Nathan in appeal. 'Is this what you really want then, love?' She smiled at him, all motherly concern, hurt by his disloyalty. 'You really want to leave me? You'd rather live with Nads and Owen, in that tiny flat?'

He knew what she was after. She wanted to agree with Brian, but she had to put Nathan in the wrong, make him sound harsh and uncaring.

He said it anyway.

'Yes. I want to go with them.'

There was a lot to sort out, back at the flat. After lunch, Owen borrowed a drill and screws from the flat below and started to rig up a hanging rail in his and Nadia's bedroom, so that they could get their clothes out of Nathan's way. Nadia said she was going to sort through the cardboard boxes and give half the stuff to the Oxfam shop.

'It'll feel more like your own room, then,' she said.

Nathan had never felt so important.

'And I must phone school to say you're living here now,' Nadia went on. 'You've been biking to school lately, haven't you? Where d'you get that bike from? It's not Smudge's, is it?'

Nathan clapped a hand over his mouth. Saskia's bike! He'd left it in the town centre yesterday afternoon, and hadn't given it a thought since.

'It's not mine. I borrowed it from Windfall. I bet someone's nicked it by now.'

'You'd better go and see.'

Nathan went round to the quiet Sunday precinct. Only a few shops were open; people had spilled from the pub to sit on the wall outside, or were eating at shaded tables outside the café. Nathan went straight to the alleyway where he'd tucked Saskia's bike yesterday. Either the alleyway was too shaded for the bike to be seen, or the bike itself was too old and decrepit for anyone to bother. Anyway, it was still there, leaning just as he'd left it. It felt like an age ago.

On an impulse, he decided to take it back up to Windfall. There was nowhere to keep it at Nadia's, other than on the street outside where anyone might take it. Besides, he felt like tidying up all the ends, for his new start. He needn't see anyone; he could just leave it by the office and then go. He mounted the bike and cycled out of town and up the hill to Coldharbour Lane.

When he got to the yard, there was no one in sight. It was still early enough for people to be having lunch. He avoided looking towards Hazel's empty pen. Tessa would be in the house; Saskia and Simon, he supposed, in their caravan. He'd never found out what they did about meals; he couldn't imagine them being domesticated enough to cook, or organise shopping. Anyway, he didn't want to see them, not when they'd conspired to take Hazel away from him.

He leaned the bike carefully against the office wall. The sun was warm on his shoulders as he walked back to the gate. The grass was splashed with white pellets of dung, and the odd loose feather. Chickens pecked around the gateway, crooning happily. Yesterday's lettuces were all planted out now, protected by chicken wire from the strong scrabbling claws of the hens.

'Nathan! Wait a minute!'

He turned round. It was Tessa, waving from Nightwalker's stable. He could have ignored her, but he walked slowly over.

'I hoped you'd come back,' she said. 'I wanted to talk to you.'

She sounded friendly enough, but he wasn't going to forget how she'd let him down over Hazel. 'What for?'

'Lots of things.' She fastened Nightwalker's

headcollar. Hooves rang on concrete as she led the big horse outside and tied him to a ring set in the wall. She had her grooming kit ready in its plastic holdall; she picked up a body brush and began grooming him with quick strokes. There was a layer of dust on the surface of the horse's coat, and underneath a deep conker sheen, silky in the sunlight.

'I'm sorry about yesterday,' Tessa said, brushing. 'I wanted to wait till it was all definite, before telling you. It's something we all have to get used to, working with animals. We can't treat them as pets. Like I told you, with that fox – it's got to fend for itself, back in the wild. Take its chances. Hazel hasn't got to take her chances. She's gone to just the right place. You need to understand that.' She looked at him. 'Especially if you're going to carry on coming up here.'

'I don't know,' Nathan mumbled.

'I hope you will. You're good with animals, and you're sensible.'

Nathan almost laughed out loud. *Sensible!* She was probably the only person in the universe who'd ever think of calling him that.

'There's just one other thing I have to warn you about.' She picked up a currycomb and ran the body brush over its teeth to clean it.

'Yeah,' Nathan said. He knew what was coming.

'That donkey. If you're going to work here, you can't go round stealing other people's animals whenever you feel like it. Whatever the circumstances,' she said firmly. 'I know it was Sue's fault—'

'Saskia's,' Nathan corrected.

'OK, Saskia's then, not yours, but you need to know. You meant well, you didn't like to see an animal neglected. But I think Simon's already explained to you that we could have called in an RSPCA inspector if you'd left the donkey where it was?'

Nathan nodded, and she went on, 'As it is, those people have got their donkey back. Perhaps they've had enough of a fright, and now they'll look after it properly. But I run this place as a business, the boarding side of it at least, and I can't afford to have people going round breaking the law, bringing stolen animals here. OK?'

'OK,' Nathan said.

Tessa relaxed her stern expression, and smiled. 'Now, if you want to keep coming up, I've decided to pay you. We'll agree on certain days and hours. Saturdays? One or two evenings? Simon won't be here much longer, and I could use some regular help. What do you think?'

'Great,' Nathan said. If he could actually earn

some money, that would help out at home. Home. For the first time in ages, he could think of Home with pride and warmth. It would help Nadia and Owen if he earned some money of his own. There was just one problem, a fairly big one. Tessa would surely change her mind once she'd heard about this.

'Er – you know what I told you, that first time I came up?' he said. 'About doing my GCSEs and being on study leave? It's – it's not true. I'm only fourteen.'

Tessa looked at him, said, 'I know,' and started brushing out Nightwalker's tail.

'You know? How?'

'Someone from your school phoned up to talk about you. Couple of weeks ago.'

Nathan stared. 'Mrs Briand?' She'd phoned two weeks ago, and Tessa still hadn't thrown him out?

'That's the one. She asked me about you, and we had quite a chat. She sounded very nice.'

Nathan stroked the soft place at the side of Nightwalker's mouth and then rubbed the whiskery nose, and the horse nuzzled him in return. He couldn't work this out.

'So what did you say?'

'I told her,' Tessa said, from the other end of Nightwalker, 'that I was perfectly happy for you to come up here. I said you were reliable, a very pleasant boy.'

Nathan gave an embarrassed laugh. He'd never heard anyone say such nice things about him as Tessa kept saying. 'I bet she nearly fell over!'

'No, she didn't sound surprised at all. You've got a very low opinion of yourself, Nathan. You should give yourself credit for your good points, you should really – there are quite a lot of them! Now, I need to look into this. There are new rules, I think, for employing fourteen-year-olds – forms to fill in. I must phone up—'

Nightwalker turned his head and stared, ears pricked, towards the gateway. A Range Rover pulled into the yard and a woman in black jodhpurs got out and walked towards the stable, giving Nightwalker an appreciative glance.

'Are you the owner?' she called to Tessa, in the manner of someone used to getting things done. 'You take stray dogs here, don't you?'

'Yes,' Tessa said.

'Good. I've got one I hope you'll be able to take,' the woman said, in her posh horsey voice. 'It's been hanging round the yard for a couple of weeks now. Thrown out, dumped by the roadside, I imagine. I can't take it on, I'm afraid, I've got Labradors of my own, so I'm rather banking on you taking it off my hands. It's a nice-looking little dog. It would be a terrible shame for it to be put to sleep.'

Nathan followed Tessa as she walked towards the Range Rover. There in the back was a small, sandy-coated terrier, squeezed into the gulley of an upturned saddle on the floor. Its ears went back as it saw the faces looking in, and its lip lifted in a snarl.

'I reported it to the police as soon as it first appeared,' said the horsey woman, 'but no one's claimed it. It's been badly treated, poor thing. Absolutely terrified. My husband and I had to trap it in a stable with some meat – simply couldn't get near it otherwise.'

The dog whimpered, and tried to press itself even more closely against the saddle.

'Poor thing. It looks petrified,' Tessa said.

'It bites if you try to handle it,' the woman said. 'You'd better wear gloves. I don't suppose you'll ever be able to rehome it.'

'We'll do our best,' Tessa said. 'It's amazing, sometimes, how they recover. Nathan, do you want to get Hazel's old place ready, while I take down details? As you see,' she added to him, rather sadly, 'there's never any shortage of ill-treated animals.'

'I'd have a go myself, but I'm afraid my Labs wouldn't stand for another dog in the house,' the woman said. She followed Tessa to the office.

Nathan went to the store for a litter-tray, feeding bowl and water-dish. Once the dog was installed, he'd spend a bit of time with it, just sitting near it. As soon as the Range Rover woman had gone, he'd ask if he could use the office phone to let Nadia and Owen know where he was and what time he'd be home.

They'd be worried about him, otherwise.

Linda Newbery
NO WAY BACK

Ellie and Amanda are best friends. Or they were, until Natalie arrived. Natalie is trouble from day one. And Ellie feels left out when Amanda starts going round with the new girl.

But then things start to go missing from the stables where Ellie works, and the finger of suspicion points at Natalie. When she makes a serious accusation against her new teacher, Ellie decides it's time to confront her.

Will Natalie back down? Will Ellie and Amanda make up and be friends again? Whatever happens there's no way back...

1 84121 582 1

£4.99

Linda Newbery
BREAK TIME

Jo loves sports, but she knows that her mum can't afford to send her on the school outdoor pursuits week. When her dad steps in and pays, her feelings are in turmoil: is he trying to buy her affection?

Angry and hurt, and determined to show her independence, Jo keeps getting into trouble.

Is now the time to break from the past?

1 84121 584 8
£4.99

More Orchard Black Apples

☐ No Way Back	*Linda Newbery*	1 84121 582 1	£4.99
☐ Break Time	*Linda Newbery*	1 84121 584 8	£4.99
☐ Revenge House	*Bernard Ashley*	1 84121 814 6	£4.99
☐ Balloon House	*Brian Keaney*	1 84121 437 X	£4.99
☐ Bitter Fruit	*Brian Keaney*	1 84121 005 6	£4.99
☐ Falling for Joshua	*Brian Keaney*	1 84121 858 8	£4.99
☐ Family Secrets	*Brian Keaney*	1 84121 530 9	£4.99
☐ Get a Life	*Jean Ure*	1 84121 831 6	£4.99
☐ Just Sixteen	*Jean Ure*	1 84121 453 1	£4.99
☐ Wolf Summer	*Andrew Matthews*	1 84121 758 1	£4.99

Orchard Black Apples are available from all good bookshops,
or can be ordered direct from the publisher:
Orchard Books, PO BOX 29, Douglas IM99 1BQ
Credit card orders please telephone 01624 836000
or fax 01624 837033
or e-mail: bookshop@enterprise.net for details.

To order please quote title, author and ISBN
and your full name and address.
Cheques and postal orders should be made payable to 'Bookpost plc.'
Postage and packing is FREE within the UK
(overseas customers should add £1.00 per book).

Prices and availability are subject to change.